PENGUIN BOOKS

Selected Short Stories

Virginia Woolf is now recognized as a major twentieth-century author, a great novelist and essayist and a key figure in literary history as a feminist and a modernist. Born in 1882, she was the daughter of the editor and critic Leslie Stephen, and suffered a traumatic adolescence after the deaths of her mother, in 1895, and her step-sister Stella, in 1897, leaving her subject to breakdowns for the rest of her life. Her father died in 1904 and two years later her favourite brother Thoby died suddenly of typhoid. With her sister, the painter Vanessa Bell, she was drawn into the company of writers and artists such as Lytton Strachey and Roger Fry, later known as the Bloomsbury Group. Among them she met Leonard Woolf, whom she married in 1912, and together they founded the Hogarth Press in 1917, which was to publish the work of T. S. Eliot, E. M. Forster and Katherine Mansfield as well as the earliest translations of Freud. Woolf lived an energetic life among friends and family, reviewing and writing, and dividing her time between London and the Sussex Downs. In 1941, fearing another attack of mental illness, she drowned herself.

Her first novel, *The Voyage Out*, appeared in 1915, and she then worked through the transitional *Night and Day* (1919) to the highly experimental and impressionistic *Jacob's Room* (1922). From then on her fiction became a series of brilliant and extraordinarily varied experiments, each one searching for a fresh way of presenting the relationship between individual lives and the forces of society and history. She was particularly concerned with women's experience, not only in her novels but also in her essays and her two books of feminist polemic, *A Room of One's Own* (1929) and *Three Guineas* (1938). Her major novels include *Mrs. Dalloway* (1925), *To the Lighthouse* (1927), the historical fantasy *Orlando* (1928), written for Vita Sackville-West, the extraordinarily poetic vision of *The Waves* (1931), the family saga of *The Years* (1937), and *Between the Acts* (1941). All these are published by Penguin, as are her *Diaries*, Volumes I–V, selections from her essays and short stories and *Flush* (1933), a reconstruction of the life of Elizabeth Barrett Browning's spaniel.

Sandra Kemp is Professor of English Literature and Cultural Theory at the University of Westminster. She writes on fiction, cultural history and literary theory. She reviews literary criticism, children's books and dance for a variety of publications. Her publications include *Kipling's Hidden Narratives*, *Italian Feminist Thought*, *Edwardian Fiction: An Oxford Companion* and *Feminisms: An Oxford Reader*. She has also edited works by Charlotte Brontë, Wilkie Collins, Rudyard Kipling, E. Nesbit, Virginia Woolf and Henry James. She is currently writing a book on portraiture.

Julia Briggs is General Editor for the works of Virginia Woolf in Penguin.

SELECTED SHORT STORIES

VIRGINIA WOOLF

EDITED WITH AN INTRODUCTION
AND NOTES BY SANDRA KEMP

PENGUIN BOOKS

PENGUIN BOOKS

Published by the Penguin Group
Penguin Books Ltd, 27 Wrights Lane, London W8 5TZ, England
Penguin Putnam Inc., 375 Hudson Street, New York, New York 10014, USA
Penguin Books Australia Ltd, Ringwood, Victoria, Australia
Penguin Books Canada Ltd, 10 Alcorn Avenue, Toronto, Ontario, Canada M4V 3B2
Penguin Books (NZ) Ltd, Private Bag 102902, NSMC, Auckland, New Zealand

Penguin Books Ltd, Registered Offices: Harmondsworth, Middlesex, England

This selection first published in Penguin Books 1993
Reprinted in Penguin Classics 2000
1 3 5 7 9 10 8 6 4 2

Set in 10.5/12.5 pt Monophoto Garamond
Typeset by Datix International Ltd, Bungay, Suffolk
Printed in England by Clays Ltd, St Ives plc

CONTENTS

Bibliographical Note

The following is a list of abbreviated titles used in this edition.

Diary: *The Diary of Virginia Woolf*, 5 vols., ed. Anne Olivier Bell (Hogarth Press, 1977; Penguin Books, 1979).

Letters: *The Letters of Virginia Woolf*, 6 vols., ed. Nigel Nicolson and Joanne Trautmann (Hogarth Press, 1975–80).

Essays: *The Essays of Virginia Woolf*, 6 vols., ed. Andrew McNeillie (Hogarth Press, 1986).

CE: *Collected Essays*, 4 vols., ed. Leonard Woolf (Chatto & Windus, 1966, 1967).

Moments of Being: *Moments of Being: Unpublished Autobiographical Writings of Virginia Woolf*, ed. Jeanne Schulkind (Hogarth Press, 1985).

Introduction

> . . . the being grows rings; identity becomes robust. What was fiery and furtive like a fling of grain cast into the air and blown hither and thither by wild gusts of life from every quarter is now methodical and orderly and flung with a purpose – so it seems.[1]

Thus Bernard, Woolf's surrogate writing self, in *The Waves*. The fragments, sketches and longer pieces that comprise Woolf's shorter fiction have a freedom from convention that the early novels ('flung with a purpose') yearned for, but dared not achieve. By contrast, the stories are 'all so casual, all so haphazard', as the narrator of 'The Mark on the Wall' remarks:

> Why, if one wants to compare life to anything, one must liken it to being blown through the Tube at fifty miles an hour – landing at the other end without a single hairpin in one's hair! Shot out at the feet of God entirely naked! Tumbling head over heels in the asphodel meadows like brown paper parcels pitched down a shoot in the post office! With one's hair flying back like the tail of a race-horse. Yes, that seems to express the rapidity of life, the perpetual waste and repair; all so casual, all so haphazard . . . (p. 54)

Woolf's shorter fiction is written against the traditional grain. It has, in her own words, more 'rhythm' than 'narrative'. She explained to Ethel Smyth, 'though the rhythmical is more natural to me than the narrative, it is completely opposed to the tradition of fiction and I am casting about all the time for some rope to throw to the reader'.[2] Yet despite its difficulties, she could not resist 'the flying phrase', and she urged her sister Vanessa to follow her example: 'I should like you to paint a large, large, picture; where everything would be brought perfectly firmly together, yet all half flying off the canvas in rapture.'[3] And Vanessa's woodcuts, which accompany the first edition of *Monday or Tuesday*, published in 1921 (and are included in this edition), are a mirror image of the stories. An anonymous reviewer in *The Times Literary Supplement* complained:

> ... the inking is often faulty; and Mrs Bell's delightful woodcuts (the one with the fiddles is peculiarly exciting and suggestive) have left ghosts of themselves on the pages opposite; and also they show through the paper, so that the backs are difficult to read.[4]

In the stories themselves, any difficulty lies in an odd combination of privacy and pace; the verve and swerve of the style inseparable from Woolf's daring experimentation with interior monologue, and her attempts, as she put it in another context, to be 'released from the cramp and confinement of personality'.[5] Another paradigm for this new narrative voice, free from conventional stylistic ties and constraints, would be the narrator's observation about Minnie in 'An Unwritten Novel':

> But when the self speaks to the self, who is speaking? – the entombed soul, the spirit driven in, in, to the central catacomb; the self that took the veil and left the world – a coward perhaps, yet somehow beautiful, as it flits with its lantern restlessly up and down dark corridors. (p. 34)

Woolf also expressed admiration for the Russian novelists, and shared with them a sense that chaotic or incoherent experience should be included in fiction. And Woolf used the stories to introduce perceptions that didn't obviously lead anywhere, or become part of a larger unit. For example, 'A Woman's College From Outside' springs out of the novel, *Jacob's Room*. But Woolf recognized that it didn't finally belong there – it moves out of the novel rather than back into it again.

Retrospectively, however, and perhaps with a degree of professional after-thought, Woolf described the process of the composition of the stories with more restraint in another letter to Ethyl Smyth:

> These little pieces in Monday or (and) Tuesday were written by way of diversion; they were the treats I allowed myself when I had done my exercise in the conventional style. I shall never forget the day I wrote The Mark on the Wall – all in a flash, as if flying, after being kept stone breaking for months. The Unwritten Novel was the great discovery, however. That – again in one second – showed me how I could embody all my deposit of experience in a shape that fitted it – not that I have ever reached that end; but anyhow I saw, branching out of the tunnel I made, when I discovered that method of approach, Jacobs Room, Mrs Dalloway etc – How I trembled with excitement; and then Leonard came in, and I drank my milk, and concealed my excitement, and wrote I suppose another page of that interminable Night and Day (which some say is my best book). All this I will tell you one day – here I suppress my natural inclination to say, if dear Ethel you have the least wish to hear any more on a subject that can't be of the least interest to you. And, I add, Green and Blue and the heron were the wild outbursts of freedom, inarticulate, ridiculous, unprintable mere outcries.[6]

'Wild outbursts of freedom' the stories may be, but the environment of *Monday or Tuesday*, and of the other short fiction, is also at once urban and banal: 'Regent Street . . . the Treaty . . . the weather not cold for the time of year, and even at that rent not a flat to be had, and the worst of influenza and its after effects' (p. 39). Woolf shared T. S. Eliot's wish to present the boredom, the horror and the reality of the everyday world rather than to construct a fictional one. 'The kiss of an old grey-haired woman with a wart on her nose' (p. 47) represents the limits of romance. And nothing happens in the stories. They are rarely 'about' anything in the conventional sense. As E. M. Forster remarked in a contemporary review of 'Kew Gardens': 'She only says, "Oh, here is something that I have seen," and then strays forward.'[7]

In a letter to George Rylands in 1934, Woolf notes that novelists from George Eliot onwards had 'lost the sense of an audience', whereas the great Victorians had displayed a sense of 'abandonment, richness, surprise, as well as a redundancy, tediousness and superficiality'.[8] In 'How Should One Read a Book?' Woolf herself defines such inclusiveness as part of the pleasure of 'rubbish reading':

> Is there not an open window on the right hand of the bookcase? How delightful to stop reading and look out! How stimulating the scene is, in its unconsciousness, its irrelevance, its perpetual movement . . . The greater part of any library is nothing but the record of such fleeting moments in the lives of men, women, and donkeys.[9]

In Woolf's view, such 'irrelevance' and 'perpetual movement' prompts a mode of response that acknowledges community between reader and writer, life and art, between 'our rush of undiscriminating emotion' and 'the swarm and confusion of life'; that attempts to capture the present moment; and that acknowledges and respects the enigma of other people: 'because one will never see them again, never know what happened next . . . as one is torn from the old lady about to pour out tea and the young man about to hit the tennis ball in the back garden of the suburban villa as one rushes past in the train' (pp. 53–4).

Elsewhere, Woolf calls this her 'little language' which echoes the old and humble 'common voice singing out of doors'.[10] Here, as Woolf explains in her essay on 'Craftsmanship', language is at its most democratic:

> Undoubtedly [words] like us to think, and they like us to feel, before we use them; but they also like us to pause; to become unconscious. Our unconsciousness is their privacy; our darkness is their light . . . That pause was made, that veil of darkness was dropped, to tempt words to come together in one of those swift marriages which are perfect images and create everlasting beauty.[11]

The 'little language' reflects a moving exchange between the personal and the impersonal, the inevitability of death, and the possibility for repeated modest human triumphs before death. 'I begin to long,' Bernard says in *The Waves*, 'for some little language such as lovers use, broken words, inarticulate words, like the shuffling of feet on the pavement':

> What is the phrase for the moon? And the phrase for love? By what name are we to call death? I do not know. I need a little language such as lovers use, words of one syllable such as children speak when they come into the room and find their mother sewing and picking up some scrap of bright wool, a feather or a shred of chintz. I need a howl; a cry . . . Nothing neat.[12]

There is nothing 'neat' about the stories. Reviewing 'Kew Gardens' in 1919, E. M. Forster admired their 'yawn and . . . gape':

> For in this queer world of Vision it is the surfaces of things, not their names or natures that matter; it has no connection with the worlds of practical or philosophic truth . . . It aims . . . at long loose sentences that sway and meander.[13]

But, for the most part, Forster's enthusiasm was only cautiously echoed by contemporary reviewers who showed themselves more comfortable with 'ordinary waking Arnold Bennett life'. In the *New Statesman* the 'Affable Hawk' proved tolerably affable:

> It is these iridescent, quickly-pricked, quickly-blown-again bubbles, made of private thoughts and dreams, which the author is an adept at describing . . . Auras, in the sense of temporary and shifting integuments of dreams and thoughts we all carry about with us while pursuing practical aims, are her subject matter . . . The contrast between the diversity and arbitrariness of the inner life and the uniformity and conventionality of the life without fills her alternately with laughter and amazement.[14]

Unsigned reviews in the *Dial* and *The Times Literary Supplement* however, were more guarded:

> The most alluring feature here is to be found in the exciting knack she has mastered of starting anywhere and arriving anywhere. But when form is vague, one has a right to ask for more frequent minor illuminations, whereas these stories too often give the effect of William Carlos Williams's *Improvisations* with the sudden flashes left out.[15]

> We complain of *Monday or Tuesday*, not that it means too little that is intelligible to the plain mind, but that it cannot help meaning

> too much for its purpose. Prose may 'aspire to the condition of music'; it cannot reach it.[16]

Today, critical opinion has not substantially changed. Woolf is still best known for her novels, and for her essays and polemics, especially *A Room of One's Own*. As she herself predicted, the stories remain 'mere tangles of words'.[17] Only the handful of stories collected by Leonard Woolf in *The Haunted House* are at all familiar. Of these, 'The New Dress' is a regular anthology piece, and 'Solid Objects' and the 'Mrs Dalloway' stories are also more widely known.

'More arty than her novels', the stories are, however, more than merely a diversion in style. Nor are they as 'difficult' or inaccessible as their critical reception would suggest. The stories are experimental, reflecting Woolf's most urgent preoccupations and the metafictional processes of her art. But they are also fun – sharp, witty, of the moment – yet memorable. Writing in her diary in 1927, Woolf noted: 'How many little stories come into my head! For instance: Ethel Sands not looking at her letters. What this implies. One might write a book of short significant scenes. She did not open her letters.'[18] Such evanescent moments – the compression of life finely into its most intense instants – determine the character, and especially the structure of the stories. They reveal what remains when 'the crumpled skin of the day [has been] cast ... into the hedge'.[19] Life is like an artist's sketch book, or snap-shots in a photo album, each moment flickers towards another. In *Monday or Tuesday*, and the later stories, the writer's mind is always alert. The characteristic 'momentary assembly of colour, sound, movement' is beautifully conveyed in the opening sequence of the 'little letter story' which became 'The Lady in the Looking-Glass'. Here the artist's eye combines the visual and the verbal:

> The room that afternoon was full of such shy creatures, lights and shadows, curtains blowing, petals falling – things that never happen, so it seems, if someone is looking ... And there were obscure flushes and darkenings too, as if a cuttlefish had suddenly

> suffused the air with purple; and the room had its passions and rages and envies and sorrows coming over it and clouding it, like a human being. Nothing stayed the same for two seconds together. (p. 75)

The story draws throughout on the reader's sensuous response, and reminds us of what Woolf described elsewhere as the loss of vision and perception in our daily lives. 'We shall very soon lose our sense of colour', she wrote in her essay on Walter Sickert; she calls this 'the worst of living in a highly organised community', and contrasts it with the responsiveness of the animal world:

> Somebody had met a man whose business it was to explore the wilder parts of the world in search of cactuses, and from him had heard of these insects who are born with the flowers and die when the flowers fade . . . At the first breath of winter . . . you might mistake them as they lay on the grass for shrivelled air-balls. Were we once insects like that, too, one of the diners asked; all eye? Do we still preserve the capacity for drinking, eating, indeed becoming colour furled up in us, waiting proper conditions to develop? For as the rocks hide fossils, so we hide tigers, baboons, and perhaps insects under our coats and hats. On first entering a picture gallery, whose stillness, warmth and seclusion from the perils of the street reproduce the conditions of the primeval forest, it often seems as if we reverted to the insect stage of our long life.[20]

In 'The Lady in the Looking-Glass', and in a number of the other stories (for example, 'An Unwritten Novel', 'Together and Apart' and 'A Summing Up'), intense moments of illumination also remind the reader (and characters) of the essentially blind isolation in which we all live. Woolf seems to suggest that the structure of the group versus the individual perhaps fits thematically with the short story which gives one individual's response rather than that of a group, as is often presented within the novel form.

In addition to being alert to their sensory associations, Woolf always linked 'moments of being' with particular scenes, and with the people who figured in them. In her unfinished autobiography Woolf linked 'scene-making' with the articulation of memory and of the past:

> In certain favourable moods, memories – what one has forgotten – come to the top. Now if this is so, is it not possible – I often wonder – that things we have felt with great intensity have an existence independent of our minds; are in fact still in existence? And if so, will it not be possible, in time, that some device will be invented by which we can tap them? I see it – the past – as an avenue lying behind; a long ribbon of scenes, emotions. There at the end of the avenue still, are the garden and the nursery.[21]

Elsewhere, Woolf described the process of 'scene-making' as her 'natural way of marking the past', 'the origin of my writing impulse'. In *To the Lighthouse* Lily remembers how Mrs Ramsay's mere presence had reconciled her to Charles Tansley: 'this scene . . . this moment of friendship and liking . . . had survived after all these years, complete, so that she dipped into it to refashion her memory of him, and it stayed in the mind almost like a work of art.'[22] The aim is to analyse the narrative forms of everyday life, 'making of the moment something permanent', capturing the way in which ordinary scenes remain fixed in the recollection:

> 'Why do they survive undamaged year after year unless they are made of something comparatively permanent? . . . in all the writing I have done, I have almost always had to make a scene when I am writing about a person; I must find a representative scene in their lives.[23]

Throughout the stories the scene-making aesthetic also figures as a framing device, crucial to considerations of harmony and balance. In *Moments of Being* Woolf describes this as 'a means of summing up and making innumerable details visible in one concrete picture.' She also develops this aesthetic in her essays. Thus, in 'Three Pictures':

> It is impossible that one should not see pictures; because if my father was a blacksmith and yours was a peer of the realm, we must needs be pictures to each other. We cannot possibly break out of the frame of the picture by speaking natural words.[24]

And in 'Impassioned Prose':

> To sit cheek by jowl with our fellows cramped up together is distasteful, indeed repulsive. But draw a little apart, see people in groups, as outlines, and they become at once memorable and full of beauty.[25]

Another letter to Ethel Smyth demonstrates that, for Woolf, the scene-making strategy was not determined by aesthetic factors alone; rather it was a matter of representing 'reality' capturing the intangible essence of a life, its 'moment of being':

> Please if ever I come again, dont meet me . . . but let me find you among your things – you cant think what a shock of emotion it gives me – seeing people among their things – I've lots such scenes in my head; the whole of life presented – the other persons life – for 10 seconds; and then it goes; and comes again; so next time dont meet me.[26]

At the end of Woolf's friendship with Vita Sackville-West, she recorded in her diary: 'Well, its like cutting off a picture: there she hangs, in the fishmongers at Sevenoaks, all pink jersey & pearls, & thats an end of it.'[27]

Reading the letters and the diary along with the stories indicates how closely related – even inextricable – are the stories and Woolf's own life. Frequently, as the letter to Ethel Smyth demonstrates above, there is a continuum from the diary, the autobiographical fragments, the letters, to a novel presented as autobiographical like *To the Lighthouse*, to the stories. (Or in the case of the genesis of the story 'Moments of Being': 'Slater's pins have no points' from 'some simple sentence' recorded in the diary, 'like Clara Pater's "Don't you find that Barker's pins have no points to them?"')[28] Woolf's attempt to blur the generic spectrum is another aspect of the extreme experimentation of her writing. In her essay on Walter Sickert, Woolf places him where she clearly sees herself, in the category of 'the hybrids':

> Among the many kinds of artists, it may be that there are some who are hybrid. Some, that is to say, bore deeper and deeper into

> the stuff of their own art; others are always making raids into the lands of others.[29]

A gloss on the stories, and on their conception, may be found in the letter to Ethel Smyth describing how she came to write the short stories, and also in the essay 'On Being Ill'. Here, as so often, Woolf shows herself ahead of her time. Both the fiction, and the non-fictional writings, reveal her concern with the links between the material nature of physical and textual 'bodies' and their expression, links that have only begun to be theorized by feminist critics in the last two decades. Woolf is interested both in the framing images, and in the imaginative possibilities behind the aesthetic distance that illness creates. She writes in that same letter to Ethel:

> One of these days I will write out some phases of my writer's life; and expound what I now merely say in short – After being ill and suffering every form and variety of nightmare and extravagant intensity of perception – for I used to make up poems, stories, profound and to me inspired phrases all day long as I lay in bed, and thus sketched, I think, all that I now, by the light of reason, try to put into prose (I thought of the Lighthouse then, and Kew and others, not in substance but in idea) . . . it composed my mind and taught me elements of composition which I should not have had the patience to learn had I been in full flush of health always.[30]

It is interesting to compare this with the poetics of sickness and the body worked out in the essay on illness where Woolf complains that there is no record of 'this daily drama of the body', because literature tries to see 'the body as a sheet of plain glass through which the soul looks straight and clear'. Instead, 'love must be deposed in favour of a temperature of 104 . . .' In the first part of the essay Woolf sets out to imagine a new genre to rival romance:

> Considering how common illness is, how tremendous the spiritual change that it brings, how astonishing, when the lights of health go down, the undiscovered countries that are then disclosed . . .

> strange indeed that illness has not taken its place with love and battle and jealousy among the prime themes of literature.[31]

Woolf contrasts the heightened states of consciousness in illness and in writing:

> Finally, to hinder the description of illness in literature, there is the poverty of the language . . . It is not only a new language that we need, more primitive, more sensual, more obscene, but a new hierarchy of the passions . . . Things are said, truths blurted out, which the cautious respectability of health conceals . . . Here we go alone, and like it better so. Always to have sympathy, always to be accompanied, always to be understood would be intolerable . . . In illness words seem to possess a mystic quality. We grasp what is beyond their surface meaning, gather instinctively this, that and the other – a sound, a colour, here a stress, there a pause . . . a state of mind which neither words can express nor the reason explain.[32]

The project of *Monday or Tuesday* is precisely to write about the life of consciousness that the Edwardian materialists had ignored. In 'The Mark on the Wall', the narrator fantasizes 'a world without professors or specialists or house-keepers with the profiles of policemen, a world in which one could slice with one's thought as a fish slices the water with his fin' (p. 58). Here the literal 'mark on the wall' also belongs to the mind:

> In certain lights that mark on the wall seems actually to project from the wall. Nor is it entirely circular. I cannot be sure, but it seems to cast a perceptible shadow, suggesting that if I ran my finger down that strip of the wall it would, at a certain point, mount and descend a small tumulus, a smooth tumulus like those barrows on the South Downs which are, they say, either tombs or camps. Of the two I should prefer them to be tombs, desiring melancholy like most English people, and finding it natural at the end of a walk to think of the bones stretched beneath the turf. (p. 57).

Throughout the shorter fiction, these lyrical exercises in the rendering of consciousness reflect the need to describe the movement of the mind and to represent different aspects of being; a new language of sensation, perception, feeling and thought. A similar aim is expressed in her essay on cinema where Woolf asks: 'Is there, we ask, some secret language which we feel and see, but never speak, and, if so, could this be made visible to the eye?'[33] In *Monday or Tuesday* and the later stories, these reveries, mood poems, or trains of thought, as they are called in 'The Mark on the Wall', are represented by a technique that Woolf anticipated in her diary: 'one thing should open out of another'. Woolf came closest to describing the challenge of reading and writing in this manner in her essay 'Three Pictures':

> It had been merely a voice. There was nothing to connect it with. No picture of any sort came to interpret it, to make it intelligible to the mind. But as the dark arose at last all one saw was an obscure human form, almost without shape, raising a gigantic arm in vain against some overwhelming iniquity.[34]

In the absence of this 'secret language' of seeing and feeling, it is the randomness of life and art, and of their connections, that is constantly present, though not always seriously. Many of the stories are parodic exercises. In 'The Mark on the Wall' and 'An Unwritten Novel', for example, there is irony in the slippage between the imaginary and the actual state of affairs:

> What has it all been about? A tree? A river? The Downs? Whitaker's Almanack? The fields of asphodel? I can't remember a thing. Everything's moving, falling, slipping, vanishing . . . There is a vast upheaval of matter. Someone is standing over me and saying –
>
> 'I'm going out to buy a newspaper.' (p. 60)

Elsewhere, there is a more serious integration of the rhythms of the human voice with the sounds and rhythms of the natural world. In *The Waves* Bernard says: 'I throw my mind out in the air as a man throws seeds in great fan-flights, falling through the purple sunset, falling on the pressed and shining plough-land which is bare.'[35] The effect is similar to the play Woolf wrote about in her diary – a play she thought of writing with 'voices speaking from the flowers'. This would be 'conceived from outside the self'.[36] So, in 'Kew Gardens':

> The ponderous woman looked through the pattern of falling words at the flowers standing cool, firm and upright in the earth, with a curious expression . . . words with short wings for their heavy body of meaning, inadequate to carry them far and thus alighting awkwardly upon the very common objects that surrounded them . . . but who knows . . . what precipices aren't concealed in them, or what slopes of ice don't shine in the sun on the other side? (pp. 50–51)

Woolf's interest in the non-human-voiced (the voice of silent objects or objects in nature) here, or elsewhere in the shorter fiction (for example, in 'A Haunted House'), shows her at her most experimental. The poeticism of short stories like these leads Woolf directly to the high modernism of the later novels (the 'Time Passes' section of *To the Lighthouse*, and the interlude sequences of *The Waves*). At the same time, Woolf clearly felt uneasy about these 'poetic' passages, as her diary shows. *Orlando* has a brief parody of 'Time Passes', and in 'An Unwritten Novel', the narrator tells us 'it's all a matter of crusts and cruets, frills and ferns' (p. 32). 'If the story's to go on gathering richness and rotundity' she tells us, it should roll 'with it two, if not three, commercial travellers and a whole grove of aspidistra' (p. 32).

In these instances, the modulation between imagined or actual reality is more than merely ironic. Time, space and the habitual associations of things are erased by this potential of the imagination.[37] In narrative terms the primacy of art over life threatens both the unity of the subject (especially the traditional notions of 'character' and 'narrator') and the bases of representation (the conventional hierarchy of people, things and events in a story). Appearances, as the adage warns, deceive. As Ruth Miller notes, the stories pun and play on the notion of 'reflection', inner and outer, reflection of the mind and of the mirror.[38] We know ourselves only through reflection, holding experience still for contemplation; we see ourselves reflected in mirrors, as figures traced across the surface of the world. Which set of images is more illusory, more deceptive? We pose for the mirror and create that momentary being who is – who reflects – the 'real' person; we go over our memories, growing ever more confused as to what is true, what imaginary. The imagination, that is, works like a mirror – reflection as a reflection; it gives us glimpses of ourselves in stories and settings that are insubstantial, caught and passed as if by bursts of sunshine. Identity is a succession of pictures.

For the narrator of 'The Mark on the Wall', the reflections of memory and imagination are, 'a matter of great importance':

> Suppose the looking glass smashes, the image disappears, and the romantic figure with the green of forest depths all about it is there no longer, but only that shell of a person which is seen by other people – what an airless, shallow, bald, prominent world it becomes! A world not to be lived in. As we face each other in omnibuses and underground railways we are looking into the mirror; that accounts for the vagueness, the gleam of glassiness, in our eyes. And the novelists in future will realize more and more the importance of these reflections, for of course there is not one reflection but an almost infinite number; those are the depths they will explore, those the phantoms they will pursue, leaving the description of reality more and more out of their stories . . . How shocking, and yet how wonderful it was to discover that these real things, Sunday luncheons, Sunday walks, country houses and tablecloths were not entirely real, were indeed half phantoms. (p. 56–7)

As if answering the question posed in 'The Mark on the Wall', 'What now takes the place of those things, I wonder, those real, standard things?' (p. 57), Woolf invests inanimate objects with a life of their own. And in all her stories, Woolf, like Bernard in *The Waves*, 'fills' her mind 'with whatever happens to be the contents of a room or a railway carriage as one fills a fountain-pen in an ink pot'.[39] Like the autonomous reflections of memory and imagination, the new status given to the objects of the outside world is another feature of Woolf's experimentation; of dismantling the old narrative hierarchies of character and plot. The stories are full of things/objects. And each thing is presented as absolutely unique, distinct from everything else. Thus in 'The Lady in the Looking-Glass':

> There were her grey-green dress, and her long shoes, her basket and something sparkling at her throat. She came so gradually that she did not seem to derange the pattern in the glass, but only to bring in some new element which gently moved and altered the other objects as if asking them, courteously, to make room for her. And the letters and the table and the grass walk and the sunflowers which had been waiting in the looking-glass separated and opened out so that she might be received among them. (p. 80)

In 'Solid Objects' the narrator's obsession with things ('thrown away, of no use to anybody, shapeless, discarded') is poignantly associated with the imagination of childhood: 'the impulse which leads a child to pick up one pebble on a path strewn with them' (p. 63). In this childish mode of perception, each object has its own character, its own possibility, defined not by its difference (or similarity) to other objects, but by its individuality. Each object is alone in the world, each object *is* the world. This way of grasping experience in its immediacy had a particular appeal for modernism. John Cage, for example, used a similar metaphor to describe the sounds in his prepared piano works: they were 'chosen as one chooses shells when walking along a beach'.[40] For Woolf, as for Cage, the artistic challenge is to perceive an object without interpreting it, to present it in itself not as standing symbolically or metaphorically for something else. 'Solid Objects' is an attempt to capture this sense of objective immediacy, this objective oddity, in words:

> Set at the opposite end of the mantlepiece from the lump of glass that had been dug from the sand, it looked like a creature from another world – freakish and fantastic as a harlequin. It seemed to be pirouetting through space, winking light like a fitful star. The

> contrast between the china so vivid and alert, and the glass so mute and contemplative, fascinated him, and wondering and amazed he asked himself how the two came to exist in the same world, let alone to stand upon the same narrow strip of marble in the same room. The question remained unanswered. (pp. 64–5)

The same dangerous autonomy is attributed to objects in 'The Mark on the Wall'. 'How readily our thoughts swarm upon a new object, lifting it a little way, as ants carry a blade of straw so feverishly, and then leave it . . . how very little control of our possessions we have . . .' muses the narrator (pp. 53–4).

In *Monday or Tuesday* and the later stories, the descriptions of rooms and houses are used to the same effect, upsetting conventional notions of character and place. In these settings rooms and furnishings aren't used to delineate human personality, but to express their refusal to be so used. The people in the stories don't leave their mark on their surroundings but are confronted with their lack of lasting impact: the empty room remains obstinately empty. It is, Woolf suggests, comforting to think that our possessions bear our traces, confirm our reality; to leave no trace to vanish, is not to have been. But objects aren't there to comfort us and, in the end, it is to their obdurate form that we must adjust. In 'The Moment: Summer's Night', the description of the family home reveals how quickly we can be boxed in:

> We . . . enter the door, and the square draws its lines around us, and here is a chair, a table, glasses, knives, and thus we are boxed and housed, and will soon require a draught of soda-water and to find something to read in bed.[41]

Throughout the stories, then, the interpenetration of life and art plays on and emphasizes the suggestiveness of reality. The world of *Monday or Tuesday* is, in Roger Fry's words, 'more real, or real with a different reality from that which we perceive in daily life'.[42] Woolf extends the boundaries of fiction not only by charting the inner life so precisely; but by this osmosis between inside and outside, self and other. And nothing in the texts allows the reader to re-establish the supremacy of what is 'real' over what is 'imaginary' (or vice versa). Art *and* life are constantly short-circuited by the invasion of each other's underlying realities.[43]

And in *Monday or Tuesday* and the later stories, art, like the present moment, does not provide a privileged position outside itself, does not enable us to determine its parameters. We occupy it, instead, as we occupy the present moment, and, in this respect, *The Times Literary Supplement* critic was right: this is prose aspiring to 'the condition of music'. What we have here is not the score – a plan for reading – but the performance itself, the immediate juxtaposition of notes. Throughout the stories Woolf deliberately blends and blurs inner and outer voices; interpretation becomes a matter of ear; 'speaks' and 'thinks' are used interchangeably. As in much other modernist fiction, the inner voice of the stories is composed of the accents and inflections of the inner life. But for Woolf this inner voice belongs neither solely to one character, nor to the narrator or dominant narrative voice. The scene that concludes Mrs Ramsay's dinner party in *To the Lighthouse* is characteristic of this doubleness:

> She did not know what they meant, but, like music, the words seemed to be spoken by her own voice, outside her self, saying quite easily and naturally what had been in her mind the whole evening while she said different things. She knew, without looking round, that everyone at the table was listening to the voice . . . with the same sort of relief and pleasure that she had, as if this were, at last, the natural thing to say, this were their own voice speaking.[44]

Woolf was perhaps correct in her own assessment of her stories. *Monday or Tuesday* and the other short fictions are indeed 'wild outbursts' – the closest she came in literature to 'flying'[45]. In 1922, Woolf wrote to Gerald Brenan: 'though I try sometimes to limit myself to the thing I do well, I am always drawn on and on, by human beings, I think, out of the little circle of safety, on and on, to the whirlpools; when I go under.'[46] One of the strongest images in the stories is the uncompromising characterization of old Miss Rashleigh and Miss Antonia in 'The

Shooting Party': 'crowing like old babies, indifferent, reckless, they laughed':

> In the deep-cut road beneath the hanger a cart stood, laid already with soft warm bodies, with limp claws, and still lustrous eyes . . . Wing, the keeper, drove the cart over the cobbles. The birds were dead now, their claws gripped tight, though they gripped nothing. The leathery eyelids were creased greyly over their eyes . . . A shot barked beneath the window . . . Light faded from the carpet. Light faded in their eyes too, as they sat by the white ashes listening. Their eyes became like pebbles, taken from water; grey stones dulled and dried. And their hands gripped their hands like the claws of dead birds gripping nothing. And they shrivelled as if the bodies inside the clothes had shrunk. Then Miss Antonia raised her glass to the mermaid. (pp. 83, 84, 87)

This later story takes us back to the starkness of Vanessa's woodcuts. No chance here of the 'simpering sweetnesses – little daisies and forget-me-nots'[47] that Woolf was so anxious to avoid. The writing escapes abstraction by being intensely physical, expressing mind through gestures of the body. 'What a little I can get down with my pen of what is so vivid to my eyes, and not only to my eyes: also to some nervous fibre or fan like membrane in my spine', Woolf wrote in her diary.[48]

In the final analysis, it seems to me that, at their best, the shorter fiction achieves what the narrator of 'The Lady in the Looking-Glass' was so anxious to describe:

> One was tired of the things that she talked about at dinner. It was her profounder state of being that one wanted to catch and turn to words, the state that is to the mind what breathing is to the body, what one calls happiness or unhappiness. (pp. 78–9)

Sandra Kemp 1993

NOTES

1. *The Waves* (1931; Penguin Books, 1992, p. 201). See also *Mrs Dalloway*: 'being laid out like a mist between the people she knew

best, who lifted her on their branches as she had seen the trees lift the mist, but it spread ever so far, her life, herself' (1925; Penguin Books, 1992, p. 10); *The Years*: 'Perhaps there's "I" at the middle of it, she thought; a knot; a centre; and again she saw herself sitting at her table drawing on the blotting-paper, digging little holes from which spokes radiated. Out and out they went . . .' (1937; Penguin Books, 1968, p. 295). The ordering impulse is even more strongly marked by Louis in *The Waves*: 'And the grinding and the steam that runs in unequal drops down the window pane; and the stopping and the starting with a jerk of motor-omnibuses; and the hesitations at counters; and the words that trail drearily with human meaning; I will reduce you to order . . . I see . . . the men in round coats perched on stools at the counter; and also behind them, eternity' (1931; Penguin Books, 1992, p. 71).

2. *Letters*, IV, 28 August 1930, p. 204; quoted by Jane Marcus in *New Feminist Essays on Virginia Woolf* (Macmillan, 1981, p. 27).
3. *Letters*, III, 5 March 1927, pp. 340–41.
4. Unsigned review, *The Times Literary Supplement*, 7 April 1921, reprinted in *Virginia Woolf: The Critical Heritage*, ed. Robin Majumdar and Allen McLaurin (Routledge & Kegan Paul, 1975, p. 88).
5. 'How It Strikes a Contemporary', reprinted in Virginia Woolf, *The Crowded Dance of Modern Life: Selected Essays, Vol. 2*, ed. Rachel Bowlby (Penguin Books, 1993, p. 29). See also, Patricia Ondek Laurence's *The Reading of Silence: Virginia Woolf in the English Tradition* (Stanford University Press, 1991, pp. 17, 217): 'Given that conventional dialogue is represented only in brief passages in a Woolf novel, and given her interest in capturing sensations, feelings and states of mind in the novel and life, what formal methods can Woolf use to portray the inner life? And since life or mind in a novel can only be written on a page, how is the inner life of the character to be represented? "What is the formal structure," as George Steiner asks in his essay "The Distribution of Discourse", of "inward speech, of the language stream we direct towards ourselves?" . . . These are difficult questions, but they are important to our understanding of Woolf, whose use of narrated monologue or "inward speech" relative to narrative "story" outweighs all modern novelists, with the exception of perhaps Marcel Proust and Nathalie Sarraute . . . If, as Gerard Genette states, silence is one of the "signs by which literature draws attention to itself and points

out its mask", then Woolf, in using silence more often than other modern authors, disturbs notions of language and narration.'

6. *Letters*, IV, 16 October 1930, p. 231.
7. 'Visions', *Daily News*, 31 July 1919 (reprinted in *VW: The Critical Heritage*, pp. 68–70). Forster's approach, through the idea of 'vision' was a useful introduction to this unusual and unEnglish kind of writing: 'A vision has nothing to do either with unreality or with edification. It is merely something that has been seen, and in this sense Mrs Woolf's two stories are visions . . . it is the world of the Eye – not of supreme importance, perhaps, but, oh, how rarely revealed! . . . [Her critics] may complain at the end that the authoress has left them where she found them. Which is, no doubt, exactly what she would wish to do.'
8. *Letters*, V, 27 September 1934, pp. 334–5.
9. *The Crowded Dance of Modern Life* (Penguin Books, 1993, p. 63).
10. 'Anon' and 'The Reader', ed. Brenda Silver, reprinted in the special Woolf issue of *Twentieth Century Literature* (vol. 25, Fall/Winter 1979, p. 382).
11. *The Crowded Dance of Modern Life* (Penguin Books, 1993, p. 143).
12. *The Waves* (1931; Penguin Books, 1992, pp. 183, 227).
13. *VW: The Critical Heritage*, p. 69.
14. *New Statesman*, 9 April 1921, p. 18 (Ibid., p. 91).
15. Unsigned review, *Dial* (New York), February 1922, vol. lxxii, no. 2 (Ibid., p. 92).
16. Ibid., pp. 87–8.
17. Phrase used in the letter to Ethel Smyth cited in Note 6, above.
18. *Diary*, III, 20 September 1927, p. 157.
19. *A Room of One's Own* (1929; reprinted with *Three Guineas*, Penguin Books, 1993, p. 22).
20. 'Walter Sickert', *CE*, II, pp. 233–4. On 18 October 1918, Roger Fry wrote to Woolf of 'The Mark on the Wall': 'You're the only one now Henry James is gone who uses language as a medium of art, who makes the very texture of the words have a meaning and quality really almost apart from what you are talking about' (quoted by Frances Spalding, *Roger Fry: Art and Life*, Granada Publishing, 1980, p. 212). In the early criticism, Woolf comes off best when her work is related to painting. For example, *The Times Literary Supplement* reviewer notes: '"Monday or Tuesday" is an example of the "unrepresentational" art which is creeping across from painting to

see what it can make of words. It sounds beautiful; it suggests beautiful, or at least life-full things – the heron flying, the busy street, the fire-lit room, and others . . .' (*VW: The Critical Heritage*, p. 87). Later criticism by A. McLaurin, *Virginia Woolf: The Echoes Enslaved* (CUP, 1973) and Harvena Richter, *Virginia Woolf: The Inward Voyage* (Princeton University Press, 1970) also sees Woolf's work in terms of, and as influenced by, painting. But it would be an oversimplification to see Woolf's writing as an *imitation* of another art form. C. Ruth Miller points out that: 'Another argument against viewing Virginia Woolf's writings as literary adaptations of paintings is that it was precisely the combination of the arts that appealed to her. Her desire was not to imitate the painter but to share his advantages while preserving her own. This eclecticism is in keeping with her vision of unity as assimilative rather than exclusive. She was attracted by the idea of a "hybrid" artist, a term she applied to Walter Sickert, who prided himself on being "a literary painter". In her critical essays, she suggests that certain writers were challenged by a divided allegiance – De Quincey, who tried to write poetry in prose, for example, or Hazlitt, who alternated between literature and painting' (*Virginia Woolf: The Frames of Art and Life*, Macmillan, 1988, p. 47).

21. *Moments of Being*, pp. 75–6.
22. *Moments of Being*, p. 156; *To the Lighthouse* (Penguin Books, 1992, p. 175, 176).
23. Here and in the quotation that follows, Jeanne Schulkind's earlier version of the text has been preferred to the revised (1985) version, cited above: *Moments of Being* (Sussex University Press, 1976, p. 122).
24. *Moments of Being* (1976 text), p. 122; *CE*, IV, p. 151.
25. *CE*, I, p. 172.
26. *Letters*, V, 18 and 19 June 1932, p. 70.
27. *Diary*, IV, 11 March 1935, p. 287.
28. *Diary*, III, 5 September 1926, p. 106.
29. *CE*, II, p. 243. In her essay *The Cinema* Woolf asked: 'Is there any characteristic which thought possesses that can be rendered visible without the help of words? It has speed and slowness; dartlike directness and vaporous circumlocution. But it has, also, especially in moments of emotion, the picture-making power, the need to lift its burden to another bearer; to let an image run side by side along

with it. The likeness of the thought is for some reason more beautiful, more comprehensible, more available than the thought itself . . . Yet if so much of our thinking and feeling is connected with seeing, some residue of visual emotion which is of no use either to painter or to poet may still await the cinema.'

30. *Letters*, IV, p. 231.
31. 'On Being Ill', *The Crowded Dance of Modern Life* (Penguin Books, 1993, pp. 43, 44, 45).
32. Ibid., pp. 44, 45, 46, 50.
33. 'The Cinema', ibid., p. 57. See also, Geoffrey Hartman in his essay 'Virginia's Web'. After quoting from *A Room of One's Own*, he observes,

 The bustle she welcomes has, at least, the arbitrariness of life rather than of the will: an errand boy here, a funeral there, business men, idlers, shoppers, each going his own way . . . Yet she is less interested in life as such than in the life of the mind which can only appear if thought is left as apparently free as the comings and goings beneath her window . . . The affirmative movement attaches itself more strongly to the slightest sign. 'Somehow it was like a signal falling, a signal pointing to a force in things which one had overlooked . . . The sight was ordinary enough. What was strange was the rhythmical order with which my imagination had invested it.' (*Beyond Formalism: Litary Essays 1958–1970*, Yale University Press, 1970, pp. 77–79).

 Woolf's vulnerability to accidental sights is also recorded in her diary: 'The squares with their regular houses & their leafless trees, & people very clearly outlined filled me with joy . . . when live people, seeming happy, produce an effect of beauty, & you don't have it offered as a work of art but it seems a natural gift of theirs, then . . . somehow it affected me as I am affected by reading Shakespeare. No: it's life' (*Diary*, II, 3 November 1923, p. 273). Likewise, after meeting Vanessa in Tottenham Court Road one day she recorded in her diary: 'Both us us sunk fathoms deep in that wash of reflection in which we both swim about . . . I was thinking a thousand things as I carried my teapot, gramophone records & stockings under my arm' (*Diary*, III, 28 March 1929, p. 219).
34. *Diary*, II, 26 January 1920, p. 13; *CE*, IV, p. 152.
35. *The Waves* (Penguin Books, 1992, p. 166).

36. *Diary*, IV, 19 January 1935, p. 275. The phrase 'conceived from outside the self' is Italo Calvino's: 'Think what it would be to have a work conceived from outside the self, a work that would never let us escape the limited perspective of the individual ego, not only to enter into selves like our own but to give speech to that which has no language, to the bird perching on the edge of the gutter, to the tree in the spring and the tree in the fall, to stones, to cement, to plastic' (*Six Memos for the Next Millennium*, trans. Patrick Creagh, Harvard University Press, 1988, p. 124), and cited by Patricia Ondek Laurence (op. cit., p. 194).
37. See *Moments of Being* (pp. 80–81), where Woolf describes how the experience of shock is for her closely allied to the sense of perceiving a pattern behind it: 'There is no Shakespeare, there is no Beethoven . . . we are the words; we are the music; we are the thing itself. And I see this when I have a shock . . . All artists I suppose feel something like this.' Compare W. B. Yeats, in the introduction to his play, *Fighting the Waves*: 'Certain typical books – *Ulysses*, Virginia Woolf's *The Waves*, Mr Ezra Pound's Draft of xxx *Cantos* – suggest a philosophy like that of the *Samkara* school of ancient India, mental and physical objects alike material, a deluge of experience breaking over us and within us, melting limits whether of line or tint; man no hard bright mirror dawdling by the dry sticks of a hedge, but a swimmer, or rather, the waves themselves. In this new literature . . . man in himself is nothing' (*Wheels and Butterflies*, Macmillan, 1934; reprinted in *W. B. Yeats: Selected Criticism and Prose*, ed. A. N. Jeffares, Macmillan, 1964, p. 210).
38. C. Ruth Miller, op. cit., pp. 96–7.
39. *The Waves* (Penguin Books, 1992, p. 50). In her *Diary* (I, 16 July 1918, p. 168), Woolf noted: 'I see why I like pictures; it's as things that stir me to describe them . . . and I insist (for the sake of my aesthetic soul) that I don't want to read stories or emotions or anything of the kind into them; only pictures that appeal to my plastic sense of words make me want to have them for still life in my novel.' She also recorded: 'Compliments, clothes, building, photography – it is for these reasons that I cannot write *Mrs Dalloway*' (*Diary*, II, 22 August 1922, p. 190).
40. Quoted in Robert P. Morgan, 'Rethinking Musical Culture', K. Bergeron and P. V. Bohlman (ed.), *Disciplining Music* (Ithaca, NY, Cornell University Press, 1990, p. 51).

41. *CE*, II, p. 297, and discussed by C. Ruth Miller (op cit., p. 81). See also E. M. Forster on *Mrs Dalloway* (*VW: The Critical Heritage*, p. 175): 'As far as her work has a message, it seems to be contained in the above paragraph. Here is one room, there another.'
42. Source not located.
43. See Daniel Ferrer, *Virginia Woolf and the Madness of Language*, translated by Geoffrey Bennington and Rachel Bowlby (Routledge, 1990, pp. 76, 75): 'This play of the fan which opens and closes . . . interposes itself and withdraws again, is a good approximation of the movement of Virginia Woolf's writing. A play of screens; of blocking and unveiling. But like a fan, this screen is complex, made up of a multitude of secondary screens which articulate and slip on to each other, are densely and deeply interleaved, and come, one at a time, to occupy the same position in the visual field. The relation between "the fundamental background" and the inessential figures behind which it is hidden is thus not a fixed point.' ('[In *The Waves*] as soon as it is named, the sun is identified with a fan – it can be closed again at any moment by the female hand holding it.')
44. *To the Lighthouse* (1927; Penguin Books, 1992, p. 120).
45. Phrases used in the letter to Ethel Smyth cited in Note 6, above.
46. *Letters*, II, 25 December 1922, p. 600.
47. Ibid., p. 599.
48. *Diary*, III, 12 August 1928, p. 191.

Further Reading

BIOGRAPHICAL

Quentin Bell, *Virginia Woolf: A biography*, 2 vols. (Hogarth Press, 1972).

Mary Ann Caws, *Women of Bloomsbury: Virginia, Vanessa and Carrington* (Routledge, 1990).

Lyndall Gordon, *Virginia Woolf: A Writer's Life* (OUP, 1984).

BIBLIOGRAPHICAL

D. T. Kirkpatrick, *A Bibliography of Virginia Woolf* (OUP, 1980).

CRITICISM

Rachel Bowlby, *Virginia Woolf: Feminist Destinations* (Blackwell, 1988).

Daniel Ferrer, *Virginia Woolf and the Madness of Language* (transl. Geoff Bennington and Rachel Bowlby, Routledge, 1990).

Patricia Ondek Laurence, *The Reading of Silence: Virginia Woolf in the English Tradition* (Stanford, 1991).

Bette London, *The Appropriated Voice: Narrative Authority in Conrad, Forster and Woolf* (Michigan, 1990).

Jane Marcus (ed.), *New Feminist Essays on Virginia Woolf* (Macmillan, 1981).

Jane Marcus (ed.), *Virginia Woolf and Bloomsbury: A Centenary Celebration* (Macmillan, 1987).

R. Majumdar and A. McLaurin (eds.), *Virginia Woolf: The Critical Heritage* (Routledge, 1975).

A. McLaurin, *Virginia Woolf: The Echoes Enslaved* (CUP, 1973).

C. Ruth Miller, *Virginia Woolf: The Frames of Art and Life* (Macmillan, 1988).

Jane Novak, *The Razor Edge of Balance: A study of Virginia Woolf* (Miami, 1975).
Harvena Richter, *Virginia Woolf, The Inward Voyage* (Princeton, 1970).
S. P. Rosenbaum, 'The Philosophical Realism of Virginia Woolf', in S. P. Rosenbaum (ed.), *English Literature and British Philosophy* (Chicago, 1971).

A Note on the Text

The text of this edition comprises the first edition of *Monday or Tuesday*, as published by the Hogarth Press in 1921; the stories are reprinted in their order of appearance within the volume and are accompanied by the original woodcuts by Woolf's sister, Vanessa Bell. The remaining stories, 'Solid Objects', 'In the Orchard', 'A Woman's College from the Outside', 'The Lady in the Looking-Glass', 'The Shooting Party', 'The Duchess and the Jeweller' and 'Lappin and Lapinova' appear here in order of their first publication, and the text follows that of their first (magazine) publication (further details are provided in the notes at the end).

SELECTED SHORT STORIES

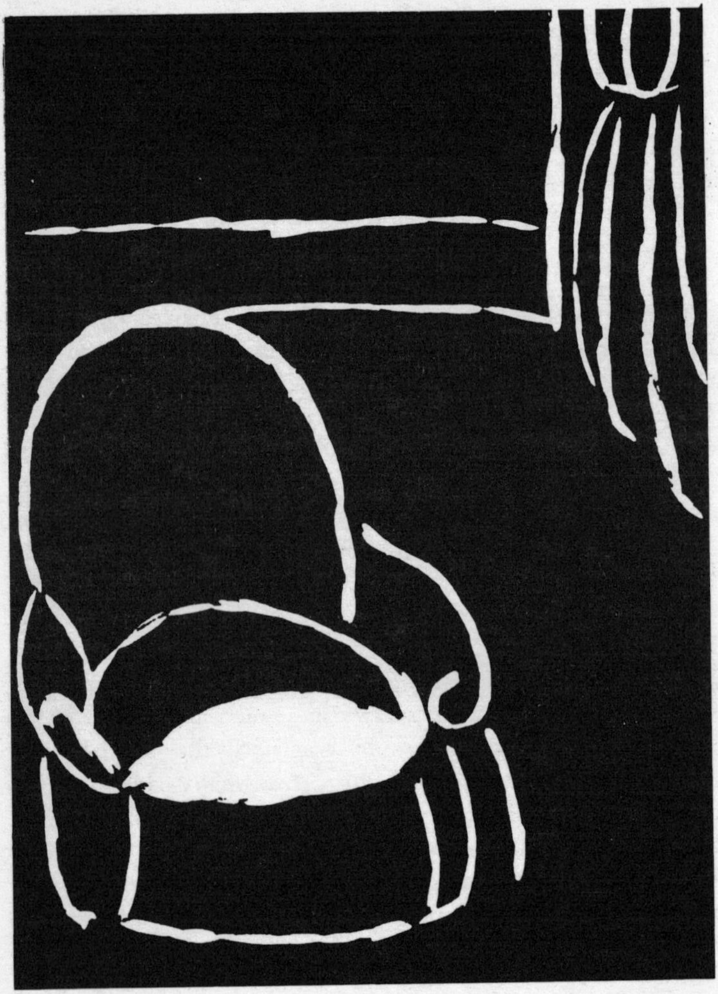

A Haunted House

Whatever hour you woke there was a door shutting. From room to room they went, hand in hand, lifting here, opening there, making sure – a ghostly couple.

'Here we left it,' she said. And he added, 'Oh, but here too!' 'It's upstairs,' she murmured. 'And in the garden,' he whispered. 'Quietly,' they said, 'or we shall wake them.'

But it wasn't that you woke us. Oh, no. 'They're looking for it; they're drawing the curtain' one might say, and so read on a page or two. 'Now they've found it,' one would be certain, stopping the pencil on the margin. And then, tired of reading, one might rise and see for oneself, the house all empty, the doors standing open, only the wood pigeons bubbling with content and the hum of the threshing machine sounding from the farm. 'What did I come in here for? What did I want to find?' My hands were empty. 'Perhaps it's upstairs then?' The apples were in the loft. And so down again, the garden still as ever, only the book had slipped into the grass.

But they had found it in the drawing-room. Not that one could ever see them. The window panes reflected apples, reflected roses; all the leaves were green in the glass. If they moved in the drawing room, the apple only turned its yellow side. Yet, the moment after, if the door was opened, spread about the floor, hung upon the walls, pendant from the ceiling – what? My hands were empty. The shadow of a thrush crossed the carpet; from the deepest wells of silence the wood pigeon drew its bubble of sound. 'Safe, safe, safe,' the pulse of the house beat softly. 'The treasure buried; the room . . .' the pulse stopped short. Oh, was that the buried treasure?

A moment later the light had faded. Out in the garden then? But the trees spun darkness for a wandering beam of sun. So fine, so rare, coolly sunk beneath the surface the beam I sought always burnt behind the glass. Death was the glass; death was between us; coming to the woman first, hundreds of years ago, leaving the house, sealing all the windows; the rooms were darkened. He left it, left her, went North, went East, saw the stars turned in the Southern sky; sought the house, found it dropped beneath the Downs. 'Safe, safe, safe,' the pulse of the house beat gladly, 'The treasure yours.'

The wind roars up the avenue. Trees stoop and bend this way and that. Moonbeams splash and spill wildly in the rain. But the beam of the lamp falls straight from the window. The candle burns stiff and still. Wandering through the house, opening the windows, whispering not to wake us, the ghostly couple seek their joy.

'Here we slept,' she says. And he adds, 'Kisses without number.' 'Waking in the morning –' 'Silver between the trees –' 'Upstairs –' 'In the garden –' 'When summer came –' 'In winter snowtime –' The doors go shutting far in the distance, gently knocking like the pulse of a heart.

Nearer they come; cease at the doorway. The wind falls, the rain slides silver down the glass. Our eyes darken; we hear no steps beside us; we see no lady spread her ghostly cloak. His hands shield the lantern. 'Look,' he breathes. 'Sound asleep. Love upon their lips.'

Stooping, holding their silver lamp above us, long they look and deeply. Long they pause. The wind drives straightly; the flame stoops slightly. Wild beams of moonlight cross both floor and wall, and, meeting, stain the faces bent; the faces pondering; the faces that search the sleepers and seek their hidden joy.

'Safe, safe, safe,' the heart of the house beats proudly. 'Long years –' he sighs. 'Again you found me.' 'Here,' she murmurs, 'sleeping; in the garden reading; laughing, rolling apples in the loft. Here we left our treasure –' Stooping, their light lifts the lids upon my eyes. 'Safe! safe! safe!' the pulse of the house beats wildly. Waking, I cry 'Oh, is *this* your buried treasure? The light in the heart.'

A Society

This is how it all came about. Six or seven of us were sitting one day after tea. Some were gazing across the street into the windows of a milliner's shop where the light still shone brightly upon scarlet feathers and golden slippers. Others were idly occupied in building little towers of sugar upon the edge of the tea tray. After a time, so far as I can remember, we drew round the fire and began as usual to praise men – how strong, how noble, how brilliant, how courageous, how beautiful they were – how we envied those who by hook or by crook managed to get attached to one for life – when Poll, who had said nothing, burst into tears. Poll, I must tell you, has always been queer. For one thing her father was a strange man. He left her a fortune in his will, but on condition that she read all the books in the London Library.[1] We comforted her as best we could; but we knew in our hearts how vain it was. For though we like her, Poll is no beauty; leaves her shoe laces untied; and must have been thinking, while we praised men, that not one of them would ever wish to marry her. At last she dried her tears. For some time we could make nothing of what she said. Strange enough it was in all conscience. She told us that, as we knew, she spent most of her time in the London Library, reading. She had begun, she said, with English literature on the top floor; and was steadily working her way down to *The Times* on the bottom. And now half, or perhaps only a quarter, way through a terrible thing had happened. She could read no more. Books were not what we thought them. 'Books' she cried, rising to her feet and speaking with an intensity of desolation which I shall never forget, 'are for the most part unutterably bad!'

Of course we cried out that Shakespeare wrote books, and Milton and Shelley.

'Oh yes,' she interrupted us. 'You've been well taught, I can see. But you are not members of the London Library.' Here her sobs broke forth anew. At length, recovering a little, she opened one of the pile of books which she always carried about with her – 'From a Window' or 'In a Garden' or some such name as that it was called, and it was written by a man called Benton or Henson[2] or something of that kind. She read the first few pages. We listened in silence. 'But that's not a book,' someone said. So she chose another. This time it was a history, but I have forgotten the writer's name. Our trepidation increased as she went on. Not a word of it seemed to be true, and the style in which it was written was execrable.

'Poetry! Poetry!' we cried, impatiently. 'Read us poetry!' I cannot describe the desolation which fell upon us as she opened a little volume and mouthed out the verbose, sentimental foolery which it contained.

'It must have been written by a woman' one of us urged. But no. She told us that it was written by a young man, one of the most famous poets of the day. I leave you to imagine what the shock of the discovery was. Though we all cried and begged her to read no more she persisted and read us extracts from the Lives of the Lord Chancellors. When she had finished, Jane, the eldest and wisest of us, rose to her feet and said that she for one was not convinced.

'Why' she asked 'if men write such rubbish as this, should our mothers have wasted their youth in bringing them into the world?'

We were all silent; and in the silence, poor Poll could be heard sobbing out, 'Why, why did my father teach me to read?'

Clorinda was the first to come to her senses. 'It's all our fault' she said. 'Every one of us knows how to read. But no one, save Poll, has ever taken the trouble to do it. I, for one, have taken it for granted that it was a woman's duty to spend her youth in bearing children. I venerated my mother for bearing ten; still more my grandmother for bearing fifteen; it was, I confess, my own ambition to bear twenty. We have gone on all these ages supposing that men were equally industrious, and that their works were of equal merit. While we have borne the child they, we supposed, have borne the books and the pictures. W have populated the world. They have civilized it. But now that we can read, what prevents us from judging the results? Before we bring another child into the world we must swear that we will find out what the world is like.'

So we made ourselves into a society for asking questions. One of us was to visit a man-of-war; another was to hide herself in a scholar's study; another was to attend a meeting of business men; while all were to read books, look at pictures, go to concerts, keep our eyes open in the streets; and ask questions perpetually. We were very young. You can judge of our simplicity when I tell you that before parting that night we agreed that the objects of life were to produce good people and good books. Our questions were to be directed to finding out how far these objects were now attained by men. We vowed solemnly that we would not bear a single child until we were satisfied.

Off we went then, some to the British Museum; others to the King's Navy; some to Oxford; others to Cambridge; we visited the Royal Academy and the Tate; heard modern music in concert rooms, went to the Law Courts, and saw new plays. No one dined out without asking her partner certain questions and carefully noting his replies. At intervals we met together and compared our observations. Oh, those were merry meetings! Never have I laughed so much as I did when Rose read her notes upon 'Honour' and described how she had dressed herself as an Ethiopian Prince and gone aboard one of His Majesty's ships.[3] Discovering the hoax, the Captain visited her (now disguised as a private gentleman) and demanded that honour should be satisfied. 'But how?' she asked. 'How?' he bellowed. 'With the cane of course!' Seeing that he was beside himself with rage and expecting that her last moment had come, she bent over and received to her amazement, six light taps upon the behind. 'The honour of the British Navy is avenged!' he cried, and, raising herself, she saw him with the sweat pouring down his face holding out a trembling right hand. 'Away!' she exclaimed, striking an attitude and imitating the ferocity of his own expression, 'My honour has still to be satisfied!' 'Spoken like a gentleman!' he returned, and fell into profound thought. 'If six strokes avenge the honour of the King's Navy' he mused, 'how many avenge the honour of a private gentleman?' He said he would prefer to lay the case before his brother officers. She replied haughtily that she could not wait. He praised her sensibility. 'Let me see,' he cried suddenly, 'did your father keep a carriage?' 'No' she said. 'Or a riding horse?' 'We had a donkey,' she bethought her, 'which drew the mowing machine.' At this his face lightened. 'My mother's name —' she added. 'For God's sake, man, don't mention your mother's name!' he shrieked, trembling like an aspen and flushing to the roots of his hair, and it was ten minutes at least before she could induce him to proceed. At length he decreed that if she gave him four strokes and a half in the small of the back at a spot indicated by himself (the half conceded, he said, in recognition of the fact that her great grandmother's uncle was killed at Trafalgar) it was his opinion that her honour would be as good as new. This was done; they retired to a restaurant; drank two bottles of wine for which he insisted upon paying; and parted with protestations of eternal friendship.

Then we had Fanny's account of her visit to the Law Courts. At her first visit she had come to the conclusion that the Judges were either made of wood or were impersonated by large animals resembling man who had been trained to move with extreme dignity, mumble and nod their heads. To test her theory she had liberated a handkerchief of bluebottles at the critical moment of a trial, but was unable to judge whether the creatures gave signs of humanity for the buzzing of the flies induced so sound a sleep that she only woke in time to see the prisoners led into the cells below. But from the evidence she brought we voted that it is unfair to suppose that the Judges are men.

Helen went to the Royal Academy, but when asked to deliver her report upon the pictures she began to recite from a pale blue volume 'O for the touch of a vanished hand and the sound of a voice that is still. Home is the hunter, home from the hill. He gave his bridle reins a shake. Love is sweet, love is brief. Spring, the fair spring, is the year's pleasant King. O! to be in England now that April's there. Men must work and women must weep. The path of duty is the way to glory –'[4] We could listen to no more of this gibberish.

'We want no more poetry!' we cried.

'Daughters of England!' she began, but here we pulled her down, a vase of water getting spilt over her in the scuffle.

'Thank God!' she exclaimed, shaking herself like a dog. 'Now I'll roll on the carpet and see if I can't brush off what remains of the Union Jack. Then perhaps –' here she rolled energetically. Getting up she began to explain to us what modern pictures are like when Castalia stopped her.

'What is the average size of a picture?' she asked. 'Perhaps two feet by two and a half,' she said. Castalia made notes while Helen spoke, and when she had done, and we were trying not to meet each others eyes, rose and said, 'At your wish I spent last week at Oxbridge, disguised as a charwoman. I thus had access to the rooms of several Professors and will now attempt to give you some idea – only,' she broke off, 'I can't think how to do it. It's all so queer. These Professors,' she went on, 'live in large houses built round grass plots each in a kind of cell by himself. Yet they have every convenience and comfort. You have only to press a button or light a little lamp. Their papers are beautifully filed. Books abound. There are no children or animals, save half a dozen stray cats and one aged bullfinch – a cock. I remember,' she broke off, 'an Aunt of mine who lived at Dulwich and kept cactuses. You reached the conservatory through the double drawing-room, and there, on the hot pipes, were dozens of them, ugly, squat, bristly little plants each in a separate pot. Once in a hundred years the Aloe flowered,[5] so my Aunt said. But she died before that happened –' We told her to keep to the point. 'Well,' she resumed, 'when Professor Hobkin was out I examined his life work, an edition of Sappho.[6] It's a queer looking book, six or seven inches thick, not all by Sappho. Oh no. Most of it is a defence of Sappho's chastity, which some German had denied, and I can assure you the passion with which these two gentlemen argued, the learning they displayed, the prodigious ingenuity with which they disputed the use of some implement which looked to me for all the world like a hairpin astounded me; especially when the door opened and Professor Hobkin himself appeared. A very nice, mild, old gentleman, but what could *he* know about chastity?' We misunderstood her.

'No, no,' she protested, 'he's the soul of honour I'm sure – not that he resembles Rose's sea captain in the least. I was thinking rather of my Aunt's cactuses. What could *they* know about chastity?'

Again we told her not to wander from the point, – did the Oxbridge professors help to produce good people and good books? – the objects of life.

'There!' she exclaimed. 'It never struck me to ask. It never occurred to me that they could possibly produce anything.'

'I believe,' said Sue, 'that you made some mistake. Probably Professor Hobkin was a gynæcologist. A scholar is a very different sort of man. A scholar is overflowing with humour and invention – perhaps addicted to wine, but what of that? – a delightful companion, generous, subtle, imaginative – as stands to reason. For he spends his life in company with the finest human beings that have ever existed.'

'Hum,' said Castalia. 'Perhaps I'd better go back and try again.'

Some three months later it happened that I was sitting alone when Castalia entered. I don't know what it was in the look of her that so moved me; but I could not restrain myself, and dashing across the room, I clasped her in my arms. Not only was she very beautiful; she seemed also in the highest spirits. 'How happy you look!' I exclaimed, as she sat down.

'I've been at Oxbridge' she said.

'Asking questions?'

'Answering them' she replied.

'You have not broken our vow?' I said anxiously, noticing something about her figure.

'Oh, the vow' she said casually. 'I'm going to have a baby if that's what you mean. You can't imagine,' she burst out, 'how exciting, how beautiful, how satisfying –'

'What is?' I asked.

'To – to – answer questions,' she replied in some confusion. Whereupon she told me the whole of her story. But in the middle of an account which interested and excited me more than anything I had ever heard, she gave the strangest cry, half whoop, half holloa –

'Chastity! Chastity! Where's my chastity!' she cried. 'Help Ho! The scent bottle!'

There was nothing in the room but a cruet containing mustard, which I was about to administer when she recovered her composure.

'You should have thought of that three months ago' I said severely.

'True' she replied. 'There's not much good in thinking of it now. It was unfortunate, by the way, that my mother had me called Castalia.'

'Oh Castalia, your mother –' I was beginning when she reached for the mustard pot.

'No, no, no,' she said, shaking her head. 'If you'd been a chaste woman yourself you would have screamed at the sight of me – instead of which you rushed across the room and took me in your arms. No, Cassandra. We are neither of us chaste.' So we went on talking.

Meanwhile the room was filling up, for it was the day appointed to discuss the results of our observations. Everyone, I thought, felt as I did about Castalia. They kissed her and said how glad they were to see her again. At length, when we were all assembled, Jane rose and said that it was time to begin. She began by saying that we had now asked questions for over five years, and that though the results were bound to be inconclusive – here Castalia nudged me and whispered that she was not so sure about that. Then she got up, and, interrupting Jane in the middle of a sentence, said,

'Before you say any more, I want to know – am I to stay in the room? Because,' she added 'I have to confess that I am an impure woman.'

Everyone looked at her in astonishment.

'You are going to have a baby?' asked Jane.

She nodded her head.

It was extraordinary to see the different expressions on their faces. A sort of hum went through the room, in which I could catch the words 'impure,' 'baby,' 'Castalia,' and so on. Jane, who was herself considerably moved, put it to us,

'Shall she go? Is she impure?'

Such a roar filled the room as might have been heard in the street outside.

'No! No! No! Let her stay! Impure? Fiddlesticks!' Yet I fancied that some of the youngest, girls of nineteen or twenty, held back as if overcome with shyness. Then we all came about her and began asking questions, and at last I saw one of the youngest, who had kept in the background, approach shyly and say to her:

'What is chastity then? I mean is it good, or is it bad, or is it nothing at all?' She replied so low that I could not catch what she said.

'You know I was shocked,' said another, 'for at least ten minutes.'

'In my opinion,' said Poll, who was growing crusty from always reading in the London Library, 'chastity is nothing but ignorance – a most discreditable state of mind. We should admit only the unchaste to our society. I vote that Castalia shall be our President.'

This was violently disputed.

'It is as unfair to brand women with chastity as with unchastity,' said Moll. 'Some of us haven't the opportunity either. Moreover, I don't believe Cassy herself maintains that she acted as she did from a pure love of knowledge.'

'He is only twenty one and divinely beautiful' said Cassy, with a ravishing gesture.

'I move,' said Helen, 'that no one be allowed to talk of chastity or unchastity save those who are in love.'

'Oh bother,' said Judith, who had been enquiring into scientific matters, 'I'm not in love and I'm longing to explain my measures for dispensing with prostitutes and fertilising virgins by Act of Parliament.'

She went on to tell us of an invention of hers to be erected at Tube Stations and other public resorts, which, upon payment of a small fee would safeguard the nation's health, accommodate its sons, and relieve its daughters. Then she had contrived a method of preserving in sealed tubes the germs of future Lord Chancellors 'or poets or painters or musicians' she went on, 'supposing, that is to say, that these breeds are not extinct, and that women still wish to bear children —'[7]

'Of course we wish to bear children!' cried Castalia impatiently. Jane rapped the table.

'That is the very point we are met to consider,' she said. 'For five years we have been trying to find out whether we are justified in continuing the human race. Castalia has anticipated our decision. But it remains for the rest of us to make up our minds.'

Here one after another of our messengers rose and delivered their reports. The marvels of civilisation far exceeded our expectations, and as we learnt for the first time how man flies in the air, talks across space, penetrates to the heart of an atom, and embraces the universe in his speculations a murmur of admiration burst from our lips.

'We are proud,' we cried, 'that our mothers sacrificed their youth in such a cause as this!' Castalia, who had been listening intently, looked prouder than all the rest. Then Jane reminded us that we had still much to learn, and Castalia begged us to make haste. On we went through a vast tangle of statistics. We learnt that England has a population of so many millions, and that such and such a proportion of them is constantly hungry and in prison; that the average size of a working man's family is such, and that so great a percentage of women die from maladies incident to childbirth. Reports were read of visits to factories, shops, slums, and dockyards. Descriptions were given of the Stock Exchange, of a gigantic house of business in the City, and of a Government Office. The British Colonies were now discussed, and some account was given of our rule in India, Africa and Ireland. I was sitting by Castalia and I noticed her uneasiness.

'We shall never come to any conclusion at all at this rate,' she said. 'As it appears that civilisation is so much more complex than we had any notion, would it not be better to confine ourselves to our original enquiry? We agreed that it was the object of life to produce good people and good books. All this time we have been talking of aeroplanes, factories and money. Let us talk about men themselves and their arts, for that is the heart of the matter.'

So the diners out stepped forward with long slips of paper containing answers to their questions. These had been framed after much consideration. A good man, we had agreed, must at any rate be honest, passionate, and unworldly. But whether or not a particular man possessed those qualities could only be discovered by asking questions, often beginning at a remote distance from the centre. Is Kensington a nice place to live in? Where is your son being educated – and your daughter? Now please tell me, what do you pay for your cigars? By the way, is Sir Joseph a baronet or only a knight? Often it seemed that we learnt more from trivial questions of this kind than from more direct ones. 'I accepted my peerage,' said Lord Bunkum 'because my wife wished it.' I forget how many titles were accepted for the same reason. 'Working fifteen hours out of the twenty-four as I do —' ten thousand professional men began.

'No, no, of course you can neither read nor write. But why do you work so hard?' 'My dear lady, with a growing family —' 'but *why* does your family grow?' 'Their wives wished that too, or perhaps it was the British Empire. But more significant than the answers were the refusals to answer. Very few would reply at all to questions about morality and religion, and such answers as were given were not serious. Questions as to the value of money and power were almost invariably brushed aside, or pressed at extreme risk to the asker. 'I'm sure,' said Jill, 'that if Sir Harley Tightboots hadn't been carving the mutton when I asked him about the capitalist system he would have cut my throat. The only reason why we escaped with our lives over and over again is that men are at once so hungry and so chivalrous. They despise us too much to mind what we say.'

'Of course they despise us' said Eleanor. 'At the same time how do you account for this – I made enquiries among the artists. Now no woman has ever been an artist, has she, Poll?'

'Jane-Austen-Charlotte-Bronte-George-Eliot,' cried Poll, like a man crying muffins in a back street.

'Damn the woman!' someone exclaimed. 'What a bore she is!'

'Since Sappho there has been no female of first rate —' Eleanor began, quoting from a weekly newspaper.

'It's now well known that Sappho was the somewhat lewd invention of Professor Hobkin,' Ruth interrupted.

'Anyhow, there is no reason to suppose that any woman ever has been able to write or ever will be able to write' Eleanor continued. 'And yet, whenever I go among authors they never cease to talk to me about their books. Masterly! I say, or Shakespeare himself! (for one must say something) and I assure you, they believe me.'

'That proves nothing,' said Jane. They all do it. 'Only,' she sighed, 'It doesn't seem to help *us* much. Perhaps we had better examine modern literature next. Liz, it's your turn.'

Elizabeth rose and said that in order to prosecute her enquiry she had dressed as a man and been taken for a reviewer.

'I have read new books pretty steadily for the past five years, said she.' 'Mr. Wells is the most popular living writer; then comes Mr. Arnold Bennett; then Mr. Compton Mackenzie; Mr. McKenna and Mr. Walpole[8] may be bracketed together.' She sat down.

'But you've told us nothing!' we expostulated. 'Or do you mean that these gentlemen have greatly surpassed Jane-Eliot and that English fiction is — where's that review of yours? Oh, yes, "safe in their hands."'

'Safe, quite safe' she said, shifting uneasily from foot to foot. 'And I'm sure that they give away even more than they receive.'

We were all sure of that. 'But,' we pressed her, 'do they write good books?'

'Good books?' she said, looking at the ceiling. 'You must remember,' she began, speaking with extreme rapidity, 'that fiction is the mirror of life. And you can't deny that education is of the highest importance, and that it would be extremely annoying, if you found yourself alone at Brighton late at night, not to know which was the best boarding house to stay at, and suppose it was a dripping Sunday evening – wouldn't it be nice to go to the Movies?'

'But what has that got to do with it?' we asked.

'Nothing – nothing – nothing whatever' she replied.

'Well, tell us the truth' we bade her.

'The truth? But isn't it wonderful,' she broke off – 'Mr. Chitter, has written a weekly article for the past thirty years upon love or hot buttered toast and has sent all his sons to Eton —'

'The truth!' we demanded.

'Oh the truth,' she stammered – 'the truth has nothing to do with literature,' and sitting down she refused to say another word.

It all seemed to us very inconclusive.

'Ladies, we must try to sum up the results' Jane was beginning, when a hum, which had been heard for some time through the open window, drowned her voice.

'War! War! War! Declaration of War!'[9] men were shouting in the street below.

We looked at each other in horror.

'What war?' we cried. 'What war?' We remembered, too late, that we had never thought of sending anyone to the House of Commons. We had forgotten all about it. We turned to Poll, who had reached the history shelves in the London Library, and asked her to enlighten us.

'Why,' we cried 'do men go to war?'

'Sometimes for one reason, sometimes for another' she replied calmly. 'In 1760, for example —' The shouts outside drowned her words. 'Again in 1797 – in 1804 – It was the Austrians in 1866 – 1870 was the Franco-Prussian – In 1900 on the other hand —'

'But it's now 1914!' we cut her short.

'Ah, I don't know what they're going to war for now,' she admitted.

The war was over and peace was in process of being signed when I once more found myself with Castalia in the room where our meetings used to be held. We began idly turning over the pages of our old minute books. 'Queer,' I mused, 'to see what we were thinking five years ago.' 'We are agreed,' Castalia quoted, reading over my shoulder, 'that it is the object to life to produce good people and good books.' We made no comment upon that. 'A good man is at any rate honest passionate and unworldly.' 'What a woman's language' I observed. 'Oh dear,' cried Castalia, pushing the book away from her, 'What fools we were! It was all Poll's father's fault,' she went on. 'I believe he did it on purpose – that ridiculous will, I mean, forcing Poll to read all the books in the London Library. If we hadn't learnt to read,' she said bitterly, 'we might still have been bearing children in ignorance and that I believe was the happiest life after all. I know what you're going to say about war,' she checked me, 'and the horror of bearing children to see them killed, but our mothers did it, and their mothers, and their mothers before them. And *they* didn't complain. They couldn't read. I've done my best,' she sighed, 'to prevent my little girl from learning to read, but what's the use? I caught Ann only yesterday with a newspaper in her hand and she was beginning to ask me if it was "true". Next she'll ask me whether Mr. Lloyd George[10] is a good man, then whether Mr. Arnold Bennett is a good novelist, and finally whether I believe in God. How can I bring my daughter up to believe in nothing?' she demanded.

'Surely you could teach her to believe that a man's intellect is, and always will be, fundamentally superior to a woman's?' I suggested. She brightened at this and began to turn over our old minutes again. 'Yes,' she said, 'think of their discoveries, their mathematics, their science, their philosophy, their scholarship —' and then she began to laugh, 'I shall never forget old Hobkin and the hairpin,' she said, and went on reading and laughing and I thought she was quite happy, when suddenly she threw the book from her and burst out, 'Oh, Cassandra why do you torment me? Don't you know that our belief in man's intellect is the greatest fallacy of them all?' 'What?' I exclaimed. 'Ask any journalist, schoolmaster, politician or public house keeper in the land and they will all tell you that men are much cleverer than women.' 'As if I doubted it,' she said scornfully. 'How could they help it? Haven't we bred them and fed and kept them in comfort since the beginning of time so that they may be clever even if they're nothing else? It's all our doing!' she cried. 'We insisted upon having intellect and now we've got it. And it's intellect,' she continued, 'that's at the bottom of it. What could be more charming than a boy before he has begun to cultivate his intellect? He is beautiful to look at; he gives himself no airs; he understands the meaning of art and literature instinctively; he goes about enjoying his life and making other people enjoy theirs. Then they teach him to cultivate his intellect. He becomes a barrister, a civil servant, a general, an author, a professor. Every day he goes to an office. Every year he produces a book. He maintains a whole family by the products of his brain — poor devil! Soon he cannot come into a room without making us all feel uncomfortable; he condescends to every woman he meets, and dares not tell the truth even to his own wife; instead of rejoicing our eyes we have to shut them if we are to take him in our arms. True, they console themselves with stars of all shapes, ribbons of all shades, and incomes of all sizes – but what is to console us? That we shall be able in ten years' time to spend a week-end at Lahore? Or that the least insect in Japan has a name twice the length of its body? Oh, Cassandra, for Heaven's sake let us devise a method by which men may bear children! It is our only chance. For unless we provide them with some innocent occupation we shall get neither good people nor good books; we shall perish beneath the fruits of their unbridled activity; and not a human being will survive to know that there once was Shakespeare!'

'It is too late,' I said. 'We cannot provide even for the children that we have.'

'And then you ask me to believe in intellect,' she said.

While we spoke, men were crying hoarsely and wearily in the street, and listening, we heard that the Treaty of Peace had just been signed.[11] The voices died away. The rain was falling and interfered no doubt with the proper explosion of the fireworks.

'My cook will have bought the *Evening News*' said Castalia 'and Ann will be spelling it out over her tea. I must go home.'

'It's no good — not a bit of good' I said. 'Once she knows how to read there's only one thing you can teach her to believe in – and that is herself.'

'Well, that would be a change,' said Castalia.

So we swept up the papers of our Society, and though Ann was playing with her doll very happily, we solemnly made her a present of the lot and told her we had chosen her to be President of the Society of the future – upon which she burst into tears, poor little girl.

Monday or Tuesday

Lazy and indifferent, shaking space easily from his wings, knowing his way, the heron passes over the church beneath the sky. White and distant, absorbed in itself, endlessly the sky covers and uncovers, moves and remains. A lake? Blot the shores of it out! A mountain? Oh, perfect – the sun gold on its slopes. Down that falls. Ferns then, or white feathers, for ever and ever —

Desiring truth, awaiting it, laboriously distilling a few words, for ever desiring – (a cry starts to the left, another to the right. Wheels strike divergently. Omnibuses conglomerate in conflict) – for ever desiring – (the clock asseverates with twelve distinct strokes that it is midday;[1] light sheds gold scales; children swarm) – for ever desiring truth. Red is the dome; coins hang on the trees; smoke trails from the chimneys; bark, shout, cry 'Iron for sale' – and truth?

Radiating to a point men's feet and women's feet, black or gold-encrusted – (This foggy weather – Sugar? No, thank you – The commonwealth of the future) – the firelight darting and making the room red, save for the black figures and their bright eyes, while outside a van discharges, Miss Thingummy drinks tea at her desk, and plate-glass preserves fur coats —

Flaunted, leaf-light, drifting at corners, blown across the wheels, silver-splashed, home or not home, gathered, scattered, squandered in separate scales, swept up, down, torn, sunk, assembled[2] – and truth?

Now to recollect by the fireside on the white square of marble. From ivory depths words rising shed their blackness, blossom and penetrate. Fallen the book; in the flame, in the smoke, in the momentary sparks – or now voyaging, the marble square pendant, minarets beneath and the India seas, while space rushes blue and stars glint – truth? or now, content with closeness?

Lazy and indifferent the heron returns; the sky veils her stars; then bares them.

An Unwritten Novel

Such an expression of unhappiness was enough by itself to make one's eyes slide above the paper's edge to the poor woman's face – insignificant without that look, almost a symbol of human destiny with it. Life's what you see in people's eyes; life's what they learn, and, having learnt it, never, though they seek to hide it, cease to be aware of – what? That life's like that, it seems. Five faces opposite – five mature faces – and the knowledge in each face. Strange, though, how people want to conceal it! Marks of reticence are on all those faces: lips shut, eyes shaded, each one of the five doing something to hide or stultify his knowledge. One smokes; another reads; a third checks entries in a pocket book; a fourth stares at the map of the line framed opposite;[1] and the fifth – the terrible thing about the fifth is that she does nothing at all. She looks at life. Ah, but my poor, unfortunate woman, do play the game – do, for all our sakes, conceal it!

As if she heard me, she looked up, shifted slightly in her seat and sighed. She seemed to apologise and at the same time to say to me, 'if only you knew!' Then she looked at life again. 'But I do know,' I answered silently, glancing at *The Times* for manners' sake: 'I know the whole business. "Peace between Germany and the Allied Powers was yesterday officially ushered in at Paris – Signor Nitti, the Italian Prime Minister[2] – a passenger train at Doncaster was in collision with a goods train . . ." We all know – *The Times* knows – but we pretend we don't.' My eyes had once more crept over the paper's rim. She shuddered, twitched her arm queerly to the middle of her back and shook her head. Again I dipped into my great reservoir of life. 'Take what you like,' I continued, 'births, deaths, marriages, Court Circular, the habits of birds, Leonardo da Vinci, the Sandhills murder, high wages and the cost of living – oh, take what you like,' I repeated, 'it's all in *The Times*!' Again with infinite weariness she moved her head from side to side until, like a top exhausted with spinning, it settled on her neck.

The Times was no protection against such sorrow as hers. But other human beings forbade intercourse. The best thing to do against life was to fold the paper so that it made a perfect square, crisp, thick, impervious even to life. This done, I glanced up quickly, armed with a shield of my own. She pierced through my shield; she gazed into my eyes as if searching any sediment of courage at the depths of them and damping it to clay. Her twitch alone denied all hope, discounted all illusion.

So we rattled through Surrey and across the border into Sussex. But with my eyes upon life I did not see that the other travellers had left, one by one, till, save for the man who read, we were alone together. Here was Three Bridges station. We drew slowly down the platform and stopped. Was he going to leave us? I prayed both ways – I prayed last that he might stay. At that instant he roused himself, crumpled his paper contemptuously, like a thing done with, burst open the door and left us alone.

The unhappy woman, leaning a little forward, palely and colourlessly addressed me – talked of stations and holidays, of brothers at Eastbourne, and the time of year, which was, I forget now, early or late. But at last looking from the window and seeing, I knew, only life, she breathed, 'Staying away – that's the drawback of it —' Ah, now we approached the catastrophe, 'My sister-in-law' – the bitterness of her tone was like lemon on cold steel, and speaking, not to me, but to herself, she muttered, 'Nonsense, she would say – that's what they all say,' and while she spoke she fidgeted as though the skin on her back were as a plucked fowl's in a poulterer's shop-window.

'Oh that cow!' she broke off nervously, as though the great wooden cow in the meadow had shocked her and saved her from some indiscretion. Then she shuddered, and then she made the awkward angular movement that I had seen before, as if, after the spasm, some spot between the shoulders burnt or itched.[3] Then again she looked the most unhappy woman in the world, and I once more reproached her, though not with the same conviction, for if there were a reason, and if I knew the reason, the stigma was removed from life.

'Sisters-in-law,' I said –

Her lips pursed as if to spit venom at the world; pursed they remained. All she did was to take her glove and rub hard at a spot on the window-pane. She rubbed as if she would rub something out for ever – some stain, some indelible contamination. Indeed, the spot remained for all her rubbing, and back she sank with the shudder and the clutch of the arm I had come to expect. Something impelled me to take my glove and rub my window. There, too, was a little speck on the glass. For all my rubbing it remained. And then the spasm went through me; I crooked my arm and plucked at the middle of my back. My skin, too, felt like the damp chicken's skin in the poulterer's shop-window; one spot between the shoulders itched and irritated, felt clammy, felt raw. Could I reach it? Surreptitiously I tried. She saw me. A smile of infinite irony, infinite sorrow, flitted and faded from her face. But she had communicated, shared her secret, passed her poison; she would speak no more. Leaning back in my corner, shielding my eyes from her eyes, seeing only the slopes and hollows, greys and purples, of the winter's landscape, I read her message, deciphered her secret, reading it beneath her gaze.

Hilda's the sister-in-law. Hilda? Hilda? Hilda Marsh – Hilda the blooming, the full bosomed, the matronly. Hilda stands at the door as the cab draws up, holding a coin. 'Poor Minnie, more of a grasshopper than ever – old cloak she had last year. Well, well, with two children these days one can't do more. No, Minnie, I've got it; here you are, cabby – none of your ways with me. Come in, Minnie. Oh, I could carry *you*, let alone your basket!' So they go into the dining-room. 'Aunt Minnie, children.'

Slowly the knives and forks sink from the upright. Down they get (Bob and Barbara), hold out hands stiffly; back again to their chairs, staring between the resumed mouthfuls. [But this we'll skip; ornaments, curtains, trefoil china plate, yellow oblongs of cheese, white squares of biscuit – skip – oh, but wait! Half-way through luncheon one of those shivers; Bob stares at her, spoon in mouth. 'Get on with your pudding, Bob;' but Hilda disapproves. 'Why *should* she twitch?' Skip, skip, till we reach the landing on the upper floor; stairs brass-bound; linoleum worn; oh yes! little bedroom looking out over the roofs of Eastbourne – zigzagging roofs like the spines of caterpillars, this way, that way, striped red and yellow, with blue-black slating]. Now, Minnie, the door's shut; Hilda heavily descends to the basement; you unstrap the straps of your basket, lay on the bed a meagre nightgown, stand side by side furred felt slippers. The looking-glass – no, you avoid the looking-glass. Some methodical disposition of hat-pins. Perhaps the shell box has something in it? You shake it; it's the pearl stud there was last year – that's all. And then the sniff, the sigh, the sitting by the window. Three o'clock on a December afternoon; the rain drizzling; one light low in the skylight of a drapery emporium; another high in a servant's bedroom – this one goes out. That gives her nothing to look at. A moment's blankness – then, what are you thinking? (Let me peep across at her opposite; she's asleep or pretending it; so what would she think about sitting at the window at three o'clock in the afternoon? Health, money, hills, her God?) Yes, sitting on the very edge of the chair looking over the roofs of Eastbourne, Minnie Marsh prays to God. That's all very well; and she may rub the pane too, as though to see God better; but what God does she see? Who's the God of Minnie Marsh, the God of the back streets of Eastbourne, the God of the three o'clock in the afternoon? I, too, see roofs, I see sky; but, oh, dear – this seeing of Gods! More like President Kruger than Prince Albert[4] – that's the best I can do for him; and I see him on a chair, in a black frock-coat, not so very high up either; I can manage a cloud or two for him to sit on; and then his hand trailing in the cloud holds a rod, a truncheon is it? – black, thick, thorned – a brutal old bully – Minnie's God! Did he send the itch and the patch and the twitch? Is that why she prays? What she rubs on the window is the stain of sin. Oh, she committed some crime!

I have my choice of crimes. The woods flit and fly – in summer there are bluebells; in the opening there, when spring comes, primroses. A parting, was it, twenty years ago? Vows broken? Not Minnie's! . . . She was faithful. How she nursed her mother! All her savings on the tombstone – wreaths under glass – daffodils in jars. But I'm off the track. A crime . . . They would say she kept her sorrow, suppressed her secret – her sex, they'd say – the scientific people. But what flummery to saddle *her* with sex! No – more like this. Passing down the streets of Croydon twenty years ago, the violet loops of ribbon in the draper's window spangled in the electric light catch her eye. She lingers – past six. Still by running she can reach home. She pushes through the glass swing door. It's sale-time. Shallow trays brim with ribbons. She pauses, pulls this, fingers that with the raised roses on it – no need to choose, no need to buy, and each tray with its surprises. 'We don't shut till seven,' and then it *is* seven. She runs, she rushes, home she reaches, but too late. Neighbours – the doctor – baby brother – the kettle – scalded – hospital – dead – or only the shock of it, the blame? Ah, but the detail matters nothing! It's what she carries with her; the spot, the crime, the thing to expiate, always there between her shoulders. 'Yes,' she seems to nod to me, 'it's the thing I did.'

Whether you did, or what you did, I don't mind; it's not the thing I want. The draper's window looped with violet – that'll do; a little cheap perhaps, a little commonplace – since one has a choice of crimes, but then so many (let me peep across again – still sleeping, or pretending sleep! white, worn, the mouth closed – a touch of obstinacy, more than one would think – no hint of sex) – so many crimes aren't *your* crime; your crime was cheap; only the retribution solemn; for now the church door opens, the hard wooden pew receives her; on the brown tiles she kneels; every day, winter, summer, dusk, dawn (here she's at it) prays. All her sins fall, fall, for ever fall. The spot receives them. It's raised, it's red, it's burning. Next she twitches. Small boys point. 'Bob at lunch to-day' – But elderly women are the worst.

Indeed now you can't sit praying any longer. Kruger's sunk beneath the clouds – washed over as with a painter's brush of liquid grey, to which he adds a tinge of black – even the tip of the truncheon gone now. That's what always happens! Just as you've seen him, felt him, someone interrupts. It's Hilda now.

How you hate her! She'll even lock the bathroom door overnight, too, though it's only cold water you want, and sometimes when the night's been bad it seems as if washing helped. And John at breakfast – the children – meals are worst, and sometimes there are friends – ferns don't altogether hide 'em – they guess too; so out you go along the front, where the waves are grey, and the papers blow, and the glass shelters green and draughty, and the chairs cost tuppence – too much – for there must be preachers along the sands. Ah, that's a nigger – that's a funny man – that's a man with parakeets – poor little creatures! Is there no one here who thinks of God? – just up there, over the pier, with his rod – but no – there's nothing but grey in the sky or if it's blue the white clouds hide him, and the music – it's military music – and what are they fishing for? Do they catch them? How the children stare! Well, then home a back way – 'Home a back way!' The words have meaning: might have been spoken by the old man with whiskers – no, no, he didn't really speak; but everything has meaning – placards leaning against doorways – names above shop-windows – red fruit in baskets – women's heads in the hairdresser's – all say 'Minnie Marsh!' But here's a jerk. 'Eggs are cheaper!' That's what always happens! I was heading her over the waterfall, straight for madness, when, like a flock of dream sheep, she turns t'other way and runs between my fingers. Eggs are cheaper. Tethered to the shores of the world, none of the crimes, sorrows, rhapsodies, or insanities for poor Minnie Marsh; never late for luncheon; never caught in a storm without a mackintosh; never utterly unconscious of the cheapness of eggs. So she reaches home – scrapes her boots.

Have I read you right? But the human face – the human face at the top of the fullest sheet of print holds more, withholds more. Now, eyes open, she looks out; and in the human eye –

how d'you define it? – there's a break – a division – so that when you've grasped the stem the butterfly's off – the moth that hangs in the evening over the yellow flower – move, raise your hand, off, high, away. I won't raise my hand. Hang still, then, quiver, life, soul, spirit, whatever you are of Minnie Marsh – I, too, on my flower – the hawk over the down – alone, or what were the worth of life? To rise; hang still in the evening, in the midday; hang still over the down. The flicker of a hand – off, up! then poised again. Alone, unseen; seeing all so still down there, all so lovely. None seeing, none caring. The eyes of others our prisons; their thoughts our cages. Air above, air below. And the moon and immortality . . . Oh, but I drop to the turf! Are you down too, you in the corner, what's your name – woman – Minnie Marsh; some such name as that? There she is, tight to her blossom; opening her hand-bag, from which she takes a hollow shell – an egg – who was saying that eggs were cheaper? You or I? Oh, it was you who said it on the way home, you remember, when the old gentleman, suddenly opening his umbrella – or sneezing was it? Anyhow, Kruger went, and you came 'home a back way,' and scraped your boots. Yes. And now you lay across your knees a pocket-handkerchief into which drop little angular fragments of eggshell – fragments of a map – a puzzle. I wish I could piece them together! If you would only sit still. She's moved her knees – the map's in bits again. Down the slopes of the Andes the white blocks of marble go bounding and hurtling, crushing to death a whole troop of Spanish muleteers, with their convoy – Drake's booty, gold and silver, But to return—

To what, to where? She opened the door, and, putting her umbrella in the stand – that goes without saying; so, too, the whiff of beef from the basement; dot, dot, dot.[5] But what I cannot thus eliminate, what I must, head down, eyes shut, with the courage of a battalion and the blindness of a bull, charge and disperse are, indubitably, the figures behind the ferns, commercial travellers. There I've hidden them all this time in the hope that somehow they'd disappear, or better still emerge, as indeed they must, if the story's to go on gathering richness and rotundity, destiny and tragedy, as stories should, rolling along with it two, if not three, commercial travellers and a whole grove of aspidistra. 'The fronds of the aspidistra only partly concealed the commercial traveller –' Rhododendrons would conceal him utterly, and into the bargain give me my fling of red and white, for which I starve and strive; but rhododendrons in Eastbourne – in December – on the Marshes' table – no, no, I dare not; it's all a matter of crusts and cruets, frills and ferns. Perhaps there'll be a moment later by the sea. Moreover, I feel, pleasantly pricking through the green fretwork and over the glacis[6] of cut glass, a desire to peer and peep at the man opposite – one's as much as I can manage. James Moggridge is it, whom the Marshes call Jimmy? [Minnie you must promise not to twitch till I've got this straight]. James Moggridge travels in – shall we say buttons? – but the time's not come for bringing *them* in – the big and the little on the long cards, some peacock-eyed, others dull gold; cairngorms some, and others coral sprays – but I say the time's not come. He travels, and on Thursdays, his Eastbourne day, takes his meals with the Marshes. His red face, his little steady eyes – by no means altogether commonplace – his enormous appetite (that's safe; he won't look at Minnie till the bread's swamped the gravy dry), napkin tucked diamond-wise – but this is primitive, and, whatever it may do the reader, don't take me in. Let's dodge to the Moggridge household, set that in motion. Well, the family boots are mended on Sundays by James himself. He reads *Truth*. But his passion? Roses – and his wife a retired hospital nurse – interesting – for God's sake let me have one woman with a name I like! But no; she's of the unborn children of the mind, illicit, none the less loved, like my rhododendrons. How many die in every novel that's written – the best, the dearest, while Moggridge lives. It's life's fault. Here's Minnie eating her egg at the moment opposite and at t'other end of the line – are we past Lewes? – there must be Jimmy – or what's her twitch for?

There must be Moggridge – life's fault. Life imposes her laws;

life blocks the way – life's behind the fern; life's the tyrant; oh, but not the bully! No, for I assure you I come willingly; I come wooed by Heaven knows what compulsion across ferns and cruets, table splashed and bottles smeared. I come irresistibly to lodge myself somewhere on the firm flesh, in the robust spine, wherever I can penetrate or find foothold on the person, in the soul, of Moggridge the man. The enormous stability of the fabric; the spine tough as whalebone, straight as oak-tree; the ribs radiating branches; the flesh taut tarpaulin; the red hollows; the suck and regurgitation of the heart; while from above meat falls in brown cubes and beer gushes to be churned to blood again – and so we reach the eyes. Behind the aspidistra they see something: black, white, dismal; now the plate again; behind the aspidistra they see elderly women; 'Marsh's sister, Hilda's more my sort;' the tablecloth now. 'Marsh would know what's wrong with Morrises . . . 'talk that over; cheese has come; the plate again; turn it round – the enormous fingers; now the woman opposite. 'Marsh's sister – not a bit like Marsh; wretched elderly female . . . You should feed your hens . . . God's truth, what's set her twitching? Not what *I* said? Dear, dear, dear! these elderly women. Dear, dear!'

'[Yes, Minnie; I know you're twitched but one moment – James Moggridge]. Dear, dear, dear!' How beautiful the sound is! like the knock of a mallet on seasoned timber, like the throb of the heart of an ancient whaler when the seas press thick and the green is clouded. 'Dear, dear!' what a passing bell for the souls of the fretful to soothe them and solace them, lap them in linen, saying, 'So long. Good luck to you!' and then, 'What's your pleasure?' for though Moggridge would pluck his rose for her, that's done, that's over. Now what's the next thing? 'Madam, you'll miss your train,' for they don't linger.

That's the man's way; that's the sound that reverberates; that's St. Paul's and the motor-omnibuses. But we're brushing the crumbs off. Oh, Moggridge, you won't stay? You must be off? Are you driving through Eastbourne this afternoon in one of those little carriages? Are you the man who's walled up in green cardboard boxes, and sometimes has the blinds down, and sometimes sits so solemn staring like a sphinx, and always there's a look of the sepulchral, something of the undertaker, the coffin, and the dusk about horse and driver? Do tell me – but the doors slammed. We shall never meet again. Moggridge, farewell!

Yes, yes, I'm coming. Right up to the top of the house. One moment I'll linger. How the mud goes round in the mind – what a swirl these monsters leave, the waters rocking, the weeds waving and green here, black there, striking to the sand, till by degrees the atoms reassemble, the deposit sifts itself, and again through the eyes one sees clear and still, and there comes to the lips some prayer for the departed, some obsequy for the souls of those one nods to, the people one never meets again.

James Moggridge is dead now, gone for ever. Well, Minnie – 'I can face it no longer.' If she said that – (Let me look at her. She is brushing the eggshell into deep declivities). She said it certainly, leaning against the wall of the bedroom, and plucking at the little balls which edge the claret-coloured curtain. But when the self speaks to the self, who is speaking? – the entombed soul, the spirit driven in, in, in to the central catacomb; the self that took the veil and left the world – a coward perhaps, yet somehow beautiful, as it flits with its lantern restlessly up and down the dark corridors. 'I can bear it no longer,' her spirit says. 'That man at lunch – Hilda – the children.' Oh, heavens, her sob! It's the spirit wailing its destiny, the spirit driven hither, thither, lodging on the diminishing carpets – meagre footholds – shrunken shreds of all the vanishing universe – love, life, faith, husband, children, I know not what splendours and pageantries glimpsed in girlhood. 'Not for me – not for me.'

But then – the muffins, the bald elderly dog? Bead mats I should fancy and the consolation of underlinen. If Minnie Marsh were run over and taken to hospital, nurses and doctors themselves would exclaim . . . There's the vista and the vision – there's the distance – the blue blot at the end of the avenue, while, after all, the tea is rich, the muffin hot, and the dog – 'Benny to your basket, sir, and see what mother's brought you!'

So, taking the glove with the worn thumb, defying once more the encroaching demon of what's called going in holes, you renew the fortifications, threading the grey wool, running it in and out.

Running it in and out, across and over, spinning a web through which God himself – hush, don't think of God! How firm the stitches are! You must be proud of your darning. Let nothing disturb her. Let the light fall gently, and the clouds show an inner vest of the first green leaf. Let the sparrow perch on the twig and shake the raindrop hanging to the twig's elbow . . . Why look up? Was it a sound, a thought? Oh, heavens! Back again to the thing you did, the plate glass with the violet loops? But Hilda will come. Ignominies, humiliations, oh! Close the breach.

Having mended her glove, Minnie Marsh lays it in the drawer. She shuts the drawer with decision. I catch sight of her face in the glass. Lips are pursed. Chin held high. Next she laces her shoes. Then she touchs her throat. What's your brooch? Mistletoe or merrythought? And what is happening? Unless I'm much mistaken, the pulse's quickened, the moments coming, the threads are racing, Niagara's ahead. Here's the crisis! Heaven be with you! Down she goes. Courage, courage! Face it, be it! For God's sake don't wait on the mat now! There's the door! I'm on your side. Speak! Confront her, confound her soul!

'Oh, I beg your pardon! Yes, this is Eastbourne. I'll reach it down for you. Let me try the handle.' [But, Minnie, though we keep up pretences, I've read you right – I'm with you now.]

'That's all your luggage?'

'Much obliged, I'm sure.'

(But why do you look about you? Hilda won't come to the station, nor John; and Moggridge is driving at the far side of Eastbourne.)

'I'll wait by my bag, ma'am, that's safest. He said he'd meet me . . . Oh, there he is! That's my son.'

So they walk off together.

Well, but I'm confounded . . . Surely Minnie, you know

better! A strange young man . . . Stop! I'll tell him – Minnie! – Miss Marsh! – I don't know though. There's something queer in her cloak as it blows. Oh, but it's untrue, it's indecent . . . Look how he bends as they reach the gateway. She finds her ticket. What's the joke? Off they go, down the road, side by side . . . Well, my world's done for! What do I stand on? What do I know? That's not Minnie. There never was Moggridge. Who am I? Life's bare as bone.

And yet the last look of them – he stepping from the kerb and she following him round the edge of the big building brims me with wonder – floods me anew. Mysterious figures! Mother and son. Who are you? Why do you walk down the street? Where to-night will you sleep, and then, to-morrow? Oh, how it whirls and surges – floats me afresh! I start after them. People drive this way and that. The white light splutters and pours. Plate-glass windows. Carnations; chrysanthemums. Ivy in dark gardens. Milk carts at the door. Wherever I go, mysterious figures, I see you, turning the corner, mothers and sons; you, you, you. I hasten, I follow. This, I fancy, must be the sea. Grey is the landscape; dim as ashes; the water murmurs and moves. If I fall on my knees, if I go through the ritual, the ancient antics, it's you, unknown figures, you I adore; if I open my arms, it's you I embrace, you I draw to me – adorable world!

The String Quartet

Well, here we are, and if you cast your eye over the room you will see that Tubes and trams and omnibuses, private carriages not a few, even, I venture to believe, landaus with bays[1] in them, have been busy at it, weaving threads from one end of London to the other. Yet I begin to have my doubts –

If indeed it's true, as they're saying, that Regent Street is up, and the Treaty signed, and the weather not cold for the time of year, and even at that rent not a flat to be had, and the worst of influenza[2] is after effects; if I bethink me of having forgotten to write about the leak in the larder, and left my glove in the train; if the ties of blood require me, leaning forward, to accept cordially the hand which is perhaps offered hesitatingly –

'Seven years since we met!'

'The last time in Venice.'

'And where are you living now?'

'Well, the late afternoon suits me the best, though, if it weren't asking too much—'

'But I knew you at once!'

'Still, the war made a break—'

If the mind's shot through by such little arrows, and — for human society compels it – no sooner is one launched than another presses forward; if this engenders heat and in addition they've turned on the electric light; if saying one thing does, in so many cases, leave behind it a need to improve and revise, stirring besides regrets, pleasures, vanities, and desires – if it's all the facts I mean, and the hats, the fur boas, the gentlemen's swallow-tail coats, and pearl tie-pins that come to the surface – what chance is there?

Of what? It becomes every minute more difficult to say why, in spite of everything, I sit here believing I can't now say what, or even remember the last time it happened.

'Did you see the procession?'

'The King looked cold.'

No, no, no. But what was it?

'She's bought a house at Malmesbury.'

'How lucky to find one!'

On the contrary, it seems to me pretty sure that she, whoever she may be, is damned, since it's all a matter of flats and hats and sea gulls, or so it seems to be for a hundred people sitting here well-dressed, walled in, furred, replete. Not that I can boast, since I too sit passive on a gilt chair, only turning the earth above a buried memory, as we all do, for there are signs, if I'm not mistaken, that we're all recalling something, furtively seeking something. Why fidget? Why so anxious about the sit of cloaks; and gloves – whether to button or unbutton? Then watch that elderly face against the dark canvas, a moment ago urbane and flushed; now taciturn and sad, as if in shadow. Was it the sound of the second violin tuning in the ante-room? Here they come; four black figures, carrying instruments, and seat themselves facing the white squares under the downpour of light; rest the tips of their bows on the music stand; with a simultaneous movement lift them; lightly poise them, and, looking across at the player opposite, the first violin counts one, two, three —

Flourish, spring, burgeon, burst! The pear tree on the top of the mountain. Fountains jet; drops descend. But the waters of the Rhone flow swift and deep, race under the arches, and sweep the trailing water leaves, washing shadows over the silver fish, the spotted fish rushed down by the swift waters, now swept into an eddy where – it's difficult this – conglomeration of fish all in a pool; leaping, splashing, scraping sharp fins; and such a boil of current that the yellow pebbles are churned round and round, round and round – free now, rushing downwards, or even somehow ascending in exquisite spirals into the air; curled like thin shavings from under a plane; up and up . . . How lovely goodness is in those who, stepping lightly, go smiling through the world! Also in old, jolly fishwives, squatted under arches, obscene old women,[3] how deeply they laugh and shake and rollick, when they walk, from side to side, hum, hah!

'That's an early Mozart, of course —'

'But the tune, like all his tunes, makes one despair – I mean hope. What do I mean? That's the worst of music! I want to dance, laugh, eat pink cakes, yellow cakes, drink thin, sharp wine. Or an indecent story, now – I could relish that. The older one grows the more one likes indecency. Hah, hah! I'm laughing. What at? You said nothing, nor did the old gentleman opposite . . . But suppose – suppose – Hush!'

The melancholy river bears us on. When the moon comes through the trailing willow boughs, I see your face, I hear your voice and the bird singing as we pass the osier bed. What are you whispering? Sorrow, sorrow. Joy, joy. Woven together[4] like reeds in moonlight. Woven together, inextricably commingled, bound in pain and strewn in sorrow — crash!

The boat sinks. Rising, the figures ascend, but now leaf thin, tapering to a dusky wraith, which, fiery tipped, draws its twofold passion from my heart. For me it sings, unseals my sorrow, thaws compassion, floods with love the sunless world, nor ceasing, abates its tenderness but deftly, subtly, weaves in and out until in this pattern, this consummation, the cleft ones unify; soar, sob, sink to rest, sorrow and joy.

Why then grieve? Ask what? Remain unsatisfied? I say all's been settled; yes; laid to rest under a coverlet of rose leaves, falling. Falling. Ah, but they cease. One rose leaf, falling from an enormous height, like a little parachute dropped from an invisible balloon, turns, flutters waveringly. It won't reach us.

'No, no. I noticed nothing. That's the worst of music – these silly dreams. The second violin was late, you say?'

'There's old Mrs. Munro, feeling her way out – blinder each year, poor woman – on this slippery floor.'

Eyeless old age, grey-headed Sphinx . . . There she stands on the pavement, beckoning, so sternly to the red omnibus.

'How lovely! How well they play! How – how – how!'

The tongue is but a clapper. Simplicity itself. The feathers in the hat next to me are bright and pleasing as a child's rattle. The leaf on the plane-tree flashes green through the chink in the curtain. Very strange, very exciting.

'How – how – how!' Hush!

These are the lovers on the grass.

'If, madam, you will take my hand —'

'Sir, I would trust you with my heart. Moreover, we have left our bodies in the banqueting hall. Those on the turf are the shadows of our souls.'

'Then these are the embraces of our souls.' The lemons nod assent. The swan pushes from the bank and floats dreaming into mid stream.

'But to return. He followed me down the corridor, and, as we turned the corner, trod on the lace of my petticoat. What could I do but cry ("Ah!") and stop to finger it? At which he drew his sword, made passes as if he were stabbing something to death, and cried, "Mad! Mad! Mad!" Whereupon I screamed, and the Prince, who was writing in the large vellum book in the oriel window, came out in his velvet skull-cap and furred slippers, snatched a rapier from the wall – the King of Spain's gift, you know – on which I escaped, flinging on this cloak to hide the ravages to my skirt – to hide . . . But listen! the horns!'

The gentleman replies so fast to the lady, and she runs up the scale with such witty exchange of compliment now culminating in a sob of passion, that the words are indistinguishable though the meaning is plain enough – love, laughter, flight, pursuit, celestial bliss – all floated out on the gayest ripple of tender endearment – until the sound of the silver horns, at first far distant, gradually sounds more and more distinctly, as if seneschals were saluting the dawn or proclaiming ominously the escape of the lovers . . . The green garden, moonlit pool, lemons, lovers, and fish are all dissolved in the opal sky, across which, as the horns are joined by trumpets and supported by clarions there rise white arches firmly planted on marble pillars . . . Tramp and trumpeting. Clang and clangour. Firm establishment. Fast foundations. March of myriads. Confusion and chaos trod to earth. But this city to which we travel has neither stone nor marble; hangs phrases thrown about not really fluid

enduring; stands unshakable; nor does a face, nor does a flag greet or welcome. Leave then to perish your hope; droop in the desert my joy; naked advance. Bare are the pillars; auspicious to none; casting no shade; resplendent; severe. Back then I fall, eager no more, desiring only to go, find the street, mark the buildings, greet the applewoman, say to the maid who opens the door: A starry night.

Change again

'Good night, good night. You go this way?'
'Alas. I go that.'

p 27

art / music sustained descrip
life - narrative - unanswered
fragmented dialogue
uncertain
concerned with direction location
achieves order

narrator part of both worlds
imagined and apparently real
impressionistic

an exercise in form
architecture
cyclical form ABCBA

woolfs description evokes
scene from Mozarts Magic Flute

music - form |AB|CDA|
|| - dialogue between people at concert

question of what is real or imagined
→ other dialogue part of an impressionism fantasy

Blue and Green

GREEN

The pointed fingers of glass hang downwards. The light slides down the glass, and drops a pool of green. All day long the ten fingers of the lustre drop green upon the marble. The feathers of parakeets – their harsh cries – sharp blades of palm trees – green too; green needles glittering in the sun. But the hard glass drips on to the marble; the pools hover above the desert sand; the camels lurch through them; the pools settle on the marble; rushes edge them; weeds clog them; here and there a white blossom; the frog flops over; at night the stars are set there unbroken. Evening comes, and the shadow sweeps the green over the mantlepiece; the ruffled surface of ocean. No ships come; the aimless waves sway beneath the empty sky. It's night; the needles drip blots of blue. The green's out.

Blue and Green

BLUE

The snub-nosed monster rises to the surface and spouts through his blunt nostrils two columns of water, which, fiery-white in the centre, spray off into a fringe of blue beads. Strokes of blue line the black tarpaulin of his hide. Slushing the water through mouth and nostrils he sinks, heavy with water, and the blue closes over him dowsing the polished pebbles of his eyes. Thrown upon the beach he lies, blunt, obtuse, shedding dry blue scales. Their metallic blue stains the rusty iron on the beach. Blue are the ribs of the wrecked rowing boat. A wave rolls beneath the blue bells. But the cathedral's different, cold, incense laden, faint blue with the veils of madonnas.

Kew Gardens

From the oval shaped flower-bed there rose perhaps a hundred stalks spreading into heart shaped or tongue shaped leaves half-way up and unfurling at the tip red or blue or yellow petals marked with spots of colour raised upon the surface; and from the red, blue or yellow gloom of the throat emerged a straight bar, rough with gold dust and slightly clubbed at the end. The petals were voluminous enough to be stirred by the summer breeze, and when they moved, the red, blue and yellow lights passed one over the other, staining an inch of the brown earth beneath with a spot of the most intricate colour. The light fell either upon the smooth grey back of a pebble, or the shell of a snail with its brown circular veins, or, falling into a raindrop, it expanded with such intensity of red, blue and yellow the thin walls of water that one expected them to burst and disappear. Instead, the drop was left in a second silver grey once more, and the light now settled upon the flesh of a leaf, revealing the branching thread of fibre beneath the surface, and again it moved on and spread its illumination in the vast green spaces beneath the dome of the heart shaped and tongue shaped leaves. Then the breeze stirred rather more briskly overhead and the colour was flashed into the air above, into the eyes of the men and women who walk in Kew Gardens in July.

The figures of these men and women straggled past the flower-bed with a curiously irregular movement not unlike that of the white and blue butterflies who crossed the turf in zig-zag flights from bed to bed. The man was about six inches in front of the woman, strolling carelessly, while she bore on with greater purpose, only turning her head now and then to see that the children were not too far behind. The man kept this distance in front of the woman purposely, though perhaps unconsciously, for he wished to go on with his thoughts.

'Fifteen years ago I came here with Lily,' he thought. 'We sat somewhere over there by a lake, and I begged her to marry me all through the hot afternoon. How the dragonfly kept circling round us: how clearly I see the dragonfly and her shoe with the square silver buckle at the toe. All the time I spoke I saw her shoe and when it moved impatiently I knew without looking up what she was going to say: the whole of her seemed to be in her shoe. And my love, my desire, were in the dragonfly; for some reason I thought that if it settled there, on that leaf, the broad one with the red flower in the middle of it if the dragonfly settled on the leaf she would say "Yes" at once. But the dragonfly went round and round: it never settled anywhere – of course not, happily not, or I shouldn't be walking here with Eleanor and the children – Tell me, Eleanor. D'you ever think of the past?'

'Why do you ask, Simon?'

'Because I've been thinking of the past. I've been thinking of Lily, the woman I might have married . . . Well, why are you silent? Do you mind my thinking of the past?'

'Why should I mind, Simon? Doesn't one always think of the past, in a garden with men and women lying under the trees? Aren't they one's past, all that remains of it, those men and women, those ghosts lying under the trees . . . one's happiness, one's reality?'

'For me, a square silver shoe buckle and a dragonfly –'

'For me, a kiss. Imagine six little girls sitting before their easels twenty years ago, down by the side of a lake, painting the water-lilies, the first red water-lilies I'd ever seen. And suddenly a kiss, there on the back of my neck. And my hand shook all the afternoon so that I couldn't paint. I took out my watch and marked the hour when I would allow myself to think of the kiss for five minutes only – it was so precious – the kiss of an old grey-haired woman with a wart on her nose, the mother of all my kisses all my life. Come Caroline, come Hubert.'

They walked on past the flower-bed, now walking four abreast, and soon diminished in size among the trees and looked half transparent as the sunlight and shade swam over their backs in large trembling irregular patches.

In the oval flower-bed the snail, whose shell had been stained red, blue, and yellow for the space of two minutes or so, now appeared to be moving very slightly in its shell, and next began to labour over the crumbs of loose earth which broke away and rolled down as it passed over them. It appeared to have a definite goal in front of it, differing in this respect from the singular high stepping angular green insect who attempted to cross in front of it, and waited for a second with its antennæ trembling as if in deliberation, and then stepped off as rapidly and strangely in the opposite direction. Brown cliffs with deep green lakes in the hollows, flat bladelike trees that waved from root to tip, round boulders of grey stone, vast crumpled surfaces of a thin crackling texture – all these objects lay across the snail's progress between one stalk and another to his goal. Before he had decided whether to circumvent the arched tent of a dead leaf or to breast it there came past the bed the feet of other human beings.

This time they were both men. The younger of the two wore an expression of perhaps unnatural calm; he raised his eyes and fixed them very steadily in front of him while his companion spoke, and directly his companion had done speaking he looked on the ground again and sometimes opened his lips only after a long pause and sometimes did not open them at all. The elder man had a curiously uneven and shaky method of walking, jerking his hand forward and throwing up his head abruptly, rather in the manner of an impatient carriage horse tired of waiting outside a house; but in the man these gestures were irresolute and pointless. He talked almost incessantly; he smiled to himself and again began to talk, as if the smile had been an answer. He was talking about spirits – the spirits of the dead, who, according to him, were even now telling him all sorts of odd things about their experiences in Heaven.

'Heaven was known to the ancients as Thessaly, William, and now, with this war, the spirit matter is rolling between the hills like thunder.' He paused, seemed to listen, smiled, jerked his head and continued –

'You have a small electric battery and a piece of rubber to insulate the wire – isolate? – insulate? – well, we'll skip the details, no good going into details that wouldn't be understood – and in short the little machine stands in any convenient position by the head of the bed, we will say, on a neat mahogany stand. All arrangements being properly fixed by workmen under my direction, the widow applies her ear and summons the spirit by sign as agreed. Women! Widows! Women in black —'

Here he seemed to have caught sight of a woman's dress in the distance, which in the shade looked a purple black. He took off his hat, placed his hand upon his heart, and hurried towards her muttering and gesticulating feverishly. But William caught him by the sleeve and touched a flower with the tip of his walking-stick in order to divert the old man's attention. After looking at it for a moment in some confusion the old man bent his ear to it and seemed to answer a voice speaking from it, for he began talking about the forests of Uruguay which he had visited hundreds of years ago in company with the most beautiful young woman in Europe. He could be heard murmuring about forests of Uruguay blanketed with the wax petals of tropical roses, nightingales, sea beaches, mermaids, and women drowned at sea,[1] as he suffered himself to be moved on by William, upon whose face the look of stoical patience grew slowly deeper and deeper.

Following his steps so closely as to be slightly puzzled by his gestures came two elderly women of the lower middle class, one stout and ponderous, the other rosy cheeked and nimble. Like most people of their station they were frankly fascinated by any signs of eccentricity betokening a disordered brain, especially in the well-to-do; but they were too far off to be certain whether the gestures were merely eccentric or genuinely mad. After they had scrutinised the old man's back in silence for a moment and given each other a queer, sly look, they went on energetically piecing together their very complicated dialogue:

'Nell, Bert, Lot, Cess, Phil, Pa, he says, I says, she says, I says, I says, I says —'

'My Bert, Sis, Bill, Grandad, the old man, sugar,

Sugar, flour, kippers, greens,
Sugar, sugar, sugar.'

The ponderous woman looked through the pattern of falling words at the flowers standing cool, firm, and upright in the earth, with a curious expression. She saw them as a sleeper waking from a heavy sleep sees a brass candlestick reflecting the light in an unfamiliar way, and closes his eyes and opens them, and seeing the brass candlestick again, finally starts broad awake and stares at the candlestick with all his powers. So the heavy woman came to a standstill opposite the oval shaped flower-bed, and ceased even to pretend to listen to what the other woman was saying. She stood there letting the words fall over her, swaying the top part of her body slowly backwards and forwards, looking at the flowers. Then she suggested that they should find a seat and have their tea.

The snail had now considered every possible method of reaching his goal without going round the dead leaf or climbing over it. Let alone the effort needed for climbing a leaf, he was doubtful whether the thin texture which vibrated with such an alarming crackle when touched even by the tip of his horns would bear his weight; and this determined him finally to creep beneath it, for there was a point where the leaf curved high enough from the ground to admit him. He had just inserted his head in the opening and was taking stock of the high brown roof and was getting used to the cool brown light when two other people came past outside on the turf. This time they were both young, a young man and a young woman. They were both in the prime of youth, or even in that season which precedes the prime of youth, the season before the smooth pink folds of the flower have burst their gummy case, when the wings of the butterfly, though fully grown, are motionless in the sun.

'Lucky it isn't Friday,' he observed.

'Why? D'you believe in luck?'

'They make you pay sixpence on Friday.'[2]

'What's sixpence anyway? Isn't it worth sixpence?'

'What's "it" – what do you mean by "it"?'

'O anything – I mean – you know what I mean.'

Long pauses came between each of these remarks; they were uttered in toneless and monotonous voices. The couple stood still on the edge of the flower-bed, and together pressed the end of her parasol deep down into the soft earth. The action and the fact that his hand rested on the top of hers expressed their feelings in a strange way, as these short insignificant words also expressed something, words with short wings for their heavy body of meaning, inadequate to carry them far and thus alighting awkwardly upon the very common objects that surrounded them, and were to their inexperienced touch so massive; but who knows (so they thought as they pressed the parasol into the earth) what precipices aren't concealed in them, or what slopes of ice don't shine in the sun on the other side? Who knows? Who has ever seen this before? Even when she wondered what sort of tea they gave you at Kew, he felt that something loomed up behind her words, and stood vast and solid behind them; and the mist very slowly rose and uncovered – O Heavens, what were those shapes? – little white tables, and waitresses who looked first at her and then at him; and there was a bill that he would pay with a real two shilling piece, and it was real, all real, he assured himself, fingering the coin in his pocket, real to everyone except to him and to her; even to him it began to seem real; and then – but it was too exciting to stand and think any longer, and he pulled the parasol out of the earth with a jerk and was impatient to find the place where one had tea with other people, like other people.

'Come along, Trissie; it's time we had our tea.'

'Wherever *does* one have one's tea?' she asked with the oddest thrill of excitement in her voice, looking vaguely round and letting herself be drawn on down the grass path, trailing her parasol, turning her head this way and that way, forgetting her tea, wishing to go down there and then down there, remembering orchids and cranes among wild flowers, a Chinese pagoda and a crimson crested bird; but he bore her on.

Thus one couple after another with much the same irregular and aimless movement passed the flower-bed and were enveloped in layer after layer of green blue vapour, in which at first their bodies had substance and a dash of colour, but later both substance and colour dissolved in the green-blue atmosphere. How hot it was! So hot that even the thrush chose to hop, like a mechanical bird, in the shadow of the flowers, with long pauses between one movement and the next; instead of rambling vaguely the white butterflies danced one above another, making with their white shifting flakes the outline of a shattered marble column above the tallest flowers; the glass roofs of the palm house shone as if a whole market full of shiny green umbrellas had opened in the sun; and in the drone of the aeroplane the voice of the summer sky murmured its fierce soul. Yellow and black, pink and snow white, shapes of all these colours, men, women, and children were spotted for a second upon the horizon, and then, seeing the breadth of yellow that lay upon the grass, they wavered and sought shade beneath the trees, dissolving like drops of water in the yellow and green atmosphere, staining it faintly with red and blue. It seemed as if all gross and heavy bodies had sunk down in the heat motionless and lay huddled upon the ground, but their voices went wavering from them as if they were flames lolling from the thick waxen bodies of candles. Voices. Yes, voices. Wordless voices, breaking the silence suddenly with such depth of contentment, such passion of desire, or, in the voices of children, such freshness of surprise; breaking the silence? But there was no silence; all the time the motor omnibuses were turning their wheels and changing their gear; like a vast nest of Chinese boxes all of wrought steel turning ceaselessly one within another the city murmured; on the top of which the voices cried aloud and the petals of myriads of flowers flashed their colours into the air.

The Mark on the Wall

Perhaps it was the middle of January in the present year that I first looked up and saw the mark on the wall. In order to fix a date it is necessary to remember what one saw. So now I think of the fire; the steady film of yellow light upon the page of my book; the three chrysanthemums in the round glass bowl on the mantelpiece. Yes, it must have been the winter time, and we had just finished our tea, for I remember that I was smoking a cigarette when I looked up and saw the mark on the wall for the first time. I looked up through the smoke of my cigarette and my eye lodged for a moment upon the burning coals, and that old fancy of the crimson flag flapping from the castle tower came into my mind, and I thought of the cavalcade of red knights riding up the side of the black rock. Rather to my relief the sight of the mark interrupted the fancy, for it is an old fancy, an automatic fancy, made as a child perhaps. The mark was a small round mark, black upon the white wall, about six or seven inches above the mantelpiece.

How readily our thoughts swarm upon a new object, lifting it a little way, as ants carry a blade of straw so feverishly, and then leave it . . . If that mark was made by a nail, it can't have been for a picture, it must have been for a miniature – the miniature of a lady with white powdered curls, powder-dusted cheeks, and lips like red carnations. A fraud of course, for the people who had this house before us would have chosen pictures in that way – an old picture for an old room. That is the sort of people they were – very interesting people, and I think of them so often, in such queer places, because one will never see them again, never know what happened next. They wanted to leave this house because they wanted to change their style of furniture, so he said, and he was in process of saying that in his opinion art should have ideas behind it when we were torn asunder, as one is torn from the old lady about to pour out tea and the young man about to hit the tennis ball in the back garden of the suburban villa as one rushes past in the train.

But as for that mark, I'm not sure about it; I don't believe it was made by a nail after all; it's too big, too round, for that. I might get up, but if I got up and looked at it, ten to one I shouldn't be able to say for certain; because once a thing's done, no one ever knows how it happened. O dear me, the mystery of life! The inaccuracy of thought! The ignorance of humanity! To show how very little control of our possessions we have – what an accidental affair this living is after all our civilisation – let me just count over a few of the things lost in one lifetime, beginning, for that seems always the most mysterious of losses – what cat would gnaw, what rat would nibble – three pale blue canisters of book-binding tools? Then there were the bird cages, the iron hoops, the steel skates, the Queen Anne coal-scuttle, the bagatelle board, the hand organ – all gone, and jewels too. Opals and emeralds, they lie about the roots of turnips. What a scraping paring affair it is to be sure! The wonder is that I've any clothes on my back, that I sit surrounded by solid furniture at this moment. Why, if one wants to compare life to anything, one must liken it to being blown through the Tube at fifty miles an hour – landing at the other end without a single hairpin in one's hair! Shot out at the feet of God entirely naked! Tumbling head over heels in the asphodel meadows[1] like brown paper parcels pitched down a shoot in the post office! With one's hair flying back like the tail of a race-horse. Yes, that seems to express the rapidity of life, the perpetual waste and repair; all so casual, all so haphazard . . .

But after life. The slow pulling down of thick green stalks so that the cup of the flower, as it turns over, deluges one with purple and red light. Why, after all, should one not be born there as one is born here, helpless, speechless, unable to focus one's eyesight, groping at the roots of the grass, at the toes of the Giants? As for saying which are trees, and which are men and women, or whether there are such things, that one won't be in a condition to do for fifty years or so. There will be nothing but spaces of light and dark, intersected by thick stalks, and rather higher up perhaps, rose-shaped blots of an indistinct colour – dim pinks and blues – which will, as times goes on, become more definite, become – I don't know what . . .

And yet that mark on the wall is not a hole at all. It may even be caused by some round black substance, such as a small rose leaf, left over from the summer, and I, not being a very vigilant housekeeper – look at the dust on the mantelpiece, for example, the dust which, so they say, buried Troy three times over, only fragments of pots utterly refusing annihilation, as one can believe.[2]

The tree outside the window taps very gently on the pane . . . I want to think quietly, calmly, spaciously, never to be interrupted, never to have to rise from my chair, to slip easily from one thing to another, without any sense of hostility, or obstacle. I want to sink deeper and deeper, away from the surface, with its hard separate facts. To steady myself, let me catch hold of the first idea that passes . . . Shakespeare . . . Well, he will do as well as another. A man who sat himself solidly in an arm-chair, and looked into the fire so – A shower of ideas fell perpetually from some very high Heaven down through his mind. He leant his forehead on his hand, and people, looking in through the open door – for this scene is supposed to take place on a summer's evening – But how dull this is, this historical fiction! It doesn't interest me at all. I wish I could hit upon a pleasant track of thought, a track indirectly reflecting credit upon myself, for those are the pleasantest thoughts, and very frequent even in the minds of modest mouse-coloured people, who believe genuinely that they dislike to hear their own praises. They are not thoughts directly praising oneself; that is the beauty of them; they are thoughts like this:

'And then I came into the room. They were discussing botany. I said how I'd seen a flower growing on a dust heap on the site of an old house in Kingsway. The seed, I said, must have been sown in the reign of Charles the First. What flowers grew in the reign of Charles the First?' I asked – (but I don't remember the answer). Tall flowers with purple tassels to them perhaps. And so it goes on. All the time I'm dressing up the figure of myself in my own mind, lovingly, stealthily, not openly adoring it, for if I did that, I should catch myself out, and stretch my hand at once for a book in self-protection. Indeed, it is curious how instinctively one protects the image of oneself from idolatry or any other handling that could make it ridiculous, or too unlike the original to be believed in any longer. Or is it not so very curious after all? It is a matter of great importance. Suppose the looking-glass smashes, the image disappears, and the romantic figure with the green of forest depths all about it is there no longer, but only that shell of a person which is seen by other people – what an airless, shallow, bald, prominent world it becomes! A world not to be lived in. As we face each other in omnibuses and underground railways we are looking into the mirror; that accounts for the vagueness, the gleam of glassiness, in our eyes. And the novelists in future will realize more and more the importance of these reflections, for of course there is not one reflection but an almost infinite number; those are the depths they will explore, those the phantoms they will pursue, leaving the description of reality more and more out of their stories, taking a knowledge of it for granted, as the Greeks did and Shakespeare perhaps – but these generalizations are very worthless. The military sound of the word is enough. It recalls leading articles, cabinet ministers – a whole class of things indeed which as a child one thought the thing itself, the standard thing, the real thing, from which one could not depart save at the risk of nameless damnation. Generalizations bring back somehow Sunday in London, Sunday afternoon walks, Sunday luncheons, and also ways of speaking of the dead, clothes, and habits – like the habit of sitting all together in one room until a certain hour, although nobody liked it. There was a rule for everything. The rule for tablecloths at that particular period was that they should be made of tapestry with little yellow compartments marked upon them, such as you may see in photographs of the carpets in the corridors of the royal palaces. Tablecloths of a different kind were not real tablecloths. How shocking, and yet how wonderful it was to discover that these real things, Sunday luncheons, Sunday walks, country houses, and tablecloths were not entirely real, were indeed half phantoms, and the damnation which visited the disbeliever in them was only a sense of illegitimate freedom. What now takes the place of those things I wonder, those real standard things? Men perhaps, should you be a woman; the masculine point of view which governs our lives, which sets the standard, which establishes Whitaker's Table of Precedency,[3] which has become, I suppose, since the war half a phantom to many men and women, which soon, one may hope, will be laughed into the dustbin where the phantoms go, the mahogany sideboards and the Landseer prints,[4] Gods and Devils, Hell and so forth, leaving us all with an intoxicating sense of illegitimate freedom – if freedom exists . . .

In certain lights that mark on the wall seems actually to project from the wall. Nor is it entirely circular. I cannot be sure, but it seems to cast a perceptible shadow, suggesting that if I ran my finger down that strip of the wall it would, at a certain point, mount and descend a small tumulus, a smooth tumulus like those barrows on the South Downs which are, they say, either tombs or camps.[5] Of the two I should prefer them to be tombs, desiring melancholy like most English people, and finding it natural at the end of a walk to think of the bones stretched beneath the turf . . . There must be some book about it. Some antiquary must have dug up those bones and given them a name . . . What sort of a man is an antiquary, I wonder? Retired Colonels for the most part, I daresay, leading parties of aged labourers to the top here, examining clods of earth and stone, and getting into correspondence with the neighbouring clergy, which, being opened at breakfast time, gives them a feeling of importance, and the comparison of arrow-heads necessitates cross-country journeys to the county towns, an agreeable necessity both to them and to their elderly wives, who wish to make plum jam or to clean out the study, and have every reason for keeping that great question of the camp or the tomb in perpetual suspension, while the Colonel himself feels agreeably philosophic in accumulating evidence on both sides of the question. It is true that he does finally incline to believe in the camp; and, being opposed, indites a pamphlet which he is about to read at the quarterly meeting of the local society when a stroke lays him low, and his last conscious thoughts are not of wife or child, but of the camp and that arrow-head there, which is now in the case at the local museum, together with the foot of a Chinese murderess, a handful of Elizabethan nails, a great many Tudor clay pipes, a piece of Roman pottery, and the wine-glass that Nelson drank out of – proving I really don't know what.

No, no, nothing is proved, nothing is known. And if I were to get up at this very moment and ascertain that the mark on the wall is really – what shall we say? – the head of a gigantic old nail, driven in two hundred years ago, which has now, owing to the patient attrition of many generations of housemaids, revealed its head above the coat of paint, and is taking its first view of modern life in the sight of a white-walled fire-lit room, what should I gain? – Knowledge? Matter for further speculation? I can think sitting still as well as standing up. And what is knowledge? What are our learned men save the descendants of witches and hermits who crouched in caves and in woods brewing herbs, interrogating shrew-mice and writing down the language of the stars? And the less we honour them as our superstitions dwindle and our respect for beauty and health of mind increases . . . Yes, one could imagine a very pleasant world. A quiet spacious world, with the flowers so red and blue in the open fields. A world without professors or specialists or house-keepers with the profiles of policemen, a world which one could slice with one's thought as a fish slices the water with his fin, grazing the stems of the water-lilies, hanging suspended over nests of white sea eggs . . . How peaceful it is down here, rooted in the centre of the world and gazing up through the gray waters, with their sudden gleams of light, and their reflections – If it were not for Whitaker's Almanack – if it were not for the Table of Precedency!

I must jump up and see for myself what that mark on the wall really is – a nail, a rose-leaf, a crack in the wood?

Here is Nature once more at her old game of self-preservation. This train of thought, she perceives, is threatening mere waste of energy, even some collision with reality, for who will ever be able to lift a finger against Whitaker's Table of Precedency? The Archbishop of Canterbury is followed by the Lord High Chancellor; the Lord High Chancellor is followed by the Archbishop of York. Everybody follows somebody, such is the philosophy of Whitaker; and the great thing is to know who follows whom. Whitaker knows, and let that, so Nature counsels, comfort you, instead of enraging you; and if you can't be comforted, if you must shatter this hour of peace, think of the mark on the wall.

I understand Nature's game – her prompting to take action as a way of ending any thought that threatens to excite or to pain. Hence, I suppose, comes our slight contempt for men of action – men, we assume, who don't think. Still, there's no harm in putting a full stop to one's disagreeable thoughts by looking at a mark on the wall.

Indeed, now that I have fixed my eyes upon it, I feel that I have grasped a plank in the sea; I feel a satisfying sense of reality which at once turns the two Archbishops and the Lord High Chancellor to the shadows of shades. Here is something definite, something real. Thus, waking from a midnight dream of horror, one hastily turns on the light and lies quiescent, worshipping the chest of drawers, worshipping solidity, worshipping reality, worshipping the impersonal world which is a proof of some existence other than ours. That is what one wants to be sure of . . . Wood is a pleasant thing to think about. It comes from a tree; and trees grow, and we don't know how they grow. For years and years they grow, without paying any attention to us, in meadows, in forests, and by the side of rivers – all things one likes to think about. The cows swish their tails beneath them on hot afternoons; they paint rivers so green that when a moorhen dives one expects to see its feathers all green when it comes up again. I like to think of the fish balanced against the stream like flags blown out; and of water-beetles slowly raising domes of mud upon the bed of the river. I like to think of the tree itself: first the close dry sensation of being wood; then the grinding of the storm; then the slow, delicious ooze of sap. I like to think of it, too, on winter's nights standing in the empty field with all leaves close-furled, nothing tender exposed to the iron bullets of the moon, a naked mast upon an earth that goes tumbling, tumbling, all night long. The song of birds must sound very loud and strange in June; and how cold the feet of insects must feel upon it, as they make laborious progresses up the creases of the bark, or sun themselves upon the thin green awning of the leaves, and look straight in front of them with diamond-cut red eyes . . . One by one the fibres snap beneath the immense cold pressure of the earth, then the last storm comes and, falling, the highest branches drive deep into the ground again. Even so, life isn't done with; there are a million patient, watchful lives still for a tree, all over the world, in bedrooms, in ships, on the pavement, lining rooms where men and women sit after tea, smoking cigarettes. It is full of peaceful thoughts, happy thoughts, this tree. I should like to take each one separately – but something is getting in the way . . . Where was I? What has it all been about? A tree? A river? The Downs? Whitaker's Almanack? The fields of asphodel? I can't remember a thing. Everything's moving, falling, slipping, vanishing . . . There is a vast upheaval of matter. Someone is standing over me and saying –

'I'm going out to buy a newspaper.'

'Yes?'

'Though it's no good buying newspapers . . . Nothing ever happens. Curse this war! God damn this war! . . . All the same, I don't see why we should have a snail on our wall.'

Ah, the mark on the wall! It was a snail.

Solid Objects

The only thing that moved upon the vast semi-circle of the beach was one small black spot. As it came nearer to the ribs and spine of the stranded pilchard boat, it became apparent from a certain tenuity in its blackness that this spot possessed four legs; and moment by moment it became more unmistakable that it was composed of the persons of two young men. Even thus in outline against the sand there was an unmistakable vitality in them; an indescribable vigour in the approach and withdrawal of the bodies, slight though it was, which proclaimed some violent argument issuing from the tiny mouths of the little round heads. This was corroborated on closer view by the repeated lunging of a walking-stick on the right-hand side. 'You mean to tell me . . . You actually believe . . .' thus the walking-stick on the right-hand side next the waves seemed to be asserting as it cut long straight stripes upon the sand.

'Politics be damned!' issued clearly from the body on the left-hand side, and, as these words were uttered, the mouths, noses, chins, little moustaches, tweed caps, rough boots, shooting coats, and check stockings of the two speakers became clearer and clearer; the smoke of their pipes went up into the air; nothing was so solid, so living, so hard, red, hirsute and virile as these two bodies for miles and miles of sea and sandhill.

They flung themselves down by the six ribs and spine of the black pilchard boat. You know how the body seems to shake itself free from an argument, and to apologize for a mood of exaltation; flinging itself down and expressing in the looseness of its attitude a readiness to take up with something new – whatever it may be that comes next to hand. So Charles, whose stick had been slashing the beach for half a mile or so, began skimming flat pieces of slate over the water; and John, who had exclaimed 'Politics be damned!' began burrowing his fingers down, down, into the sand. As his hand went further and further beyond the wrist, so that he had to hitch his sleeve a little higher, his eyes lost their intensity, or rather the background of thought and experience which gives an inscrutable depth to the eyes of grown people disappeared, leaving only the clear transparent surface, expressing nothing but wonder, which the eyes of young children display. No doubt the act of burrowing in the sand had something to do with it. He remembered that, after digging for a little, the water oozes round your finger-tips; the hole then becomes a moat; a well; a spring; a secret channel to the sea. As he was choosing which of these things to make it, still working his fingers in the water, they curled round something hard – a full drop of solid matter – and gradually dislodged a large irregular lump, and brought it to the surface. When the sand coating was wiped off, a green tint appeared. It was a lump of glass, so thick as to be almost opaque; the smoothing of the sea had completely worn off any edge or shape, so that it was impossible to say whether it had been bottle, tumbler or window-pane; it was nothing but glass; it was almost a precious stone. You had only to enclose it in a rim of gold, or pierce it with a wire, and it became a jewel; part of a necklace, or a dull, green light upon a finger. Perhaps after all it was really a gem; something worn by a dark Princess trailing her finger in the water as she sat in the stern of the boat and listened to the slaves singing as they rowed her across the Bay. Or the oak sides of a sunk Elizabethan treasure-chest had split apart, and, rolled over and over, over and over, its emeralds had come at last to shore. John turned it in his hands; he held it to the light; he held it so that its irregular mass blotted out the body and extended right arm of his friend. The green thinned and thickened slightly as it was held against the sky or against the body. It pleased him; it puzzled him; it was so hard, so concentrated, so definite an object compared with the vague sea and the hazy shore.

Now a sigh disturbed him – profound, final, making him aware that his friend Charles had thrown all the flat stones within reach, or had come to the conclusion that it was not worth while to throw them. They ate their sandwiches side by side. When they had done, and were shaking themselves and rising to their feet, John took the lump of glass and looked at it in silence. Charles looked at it too. But he saw immediately that it was not flat, and filling his pipe he said with the energy that dismisses a foolish strain of thought,

'To return to what I was saying —'

He did not see, or if he had seen would hardly have noticed, that John after looking at the lump for a moment, as if in hesitation, slipped it inside his pocket. That impulse, too, may have been the impulse which leads a child to pick up one pebble on a path strewn with them, promising it a life of warmth and security upon the nursery mantelpiece, delighting in the sense of power and benignity which such an action confers, and believing that the heart of the stone leaps with joy when it sees itself chosen from a million like it, to enjoy this bliss instead of a life of cold and wet upon the high road. 'It might so easily have been any other of the millions of stones, but it was I, I, I!'

Whether this thought or not was in John's mind: the lump of glass had its place upon the mantelpiece, where it stood heavy upon a little pile of bills and letters, and served not only as an excellent paper-weight, but also as a natural stopping place for the young man's eyes when they wandered from his book. Looked at again and again half consciously by a mind thinking of something else, any object mixes itself so profoundly with the stuff of thought that it loses its actual form and recomposes itself a little differently in an ideal shape which haunts the brain when we least expect it. So John found himself attracted to the windows of curiosity shops when he was out walking, merely because he saw something which reminded him of the lump of glass. Anything, so long as it was an object of some kind, more or less round, perhaps with a dying flame deep sunk in its mass, anything – china, glass, amber, rock, marble – even the smooth oval egg of a prehistoric bird would do. He took, also, to keeping his eyes upon the ground, especially in the neighbourhood of waste land where the household refuse is thrown away.

Such objects often occurred there – thrown away, of no use to anybody, shapeless, discarded. In a few months he had collected four or five specimens that took their place upon the mantelpiece. They were useful, too, for a man who is standing for Parliament upon the brink of a brilliant career has any number of papers to keep in order – addresses to constituents, declarations of policy, appeals for subscriptions, invitations to dinner, and so on.

One day, starting from his rooms in the Temple to catch a train in order to address his constituents, his eyes rested upon a remarkable object lying half-hidden in one of those little borders of grass which edge the bases of vast legal buildings. He could only touch it with the point of his stick through the railings; but he could see that it was a piece of china of the most remarkable shape, as nearly resembling a starfish as anything – shaped, or broken accidentally, into five irregular but unmistakable points. The colouring was mainly blue, but green stripes or spots of some kind overlaid the blue, and lines of crimson gave it a richness and lustre of the most attractive kind. John was determined to possess it; but the more he pushed, the further it receded. At length he was forced to go back to his rooms and improvise a wire ring attached to the end of a stick, with which, by dint of great care and skill, he finally drew the piece of china within reach of his hands. As he seized hold of it he exclaimed in triumph. At that moment the clock struck. It was out of the question that he should keep his appointment. The meeting was held without him. But how had the piece of china been broken into this remarkable shape? A careful examination put it beyond doubt that the star shape was accidental, which made it all the more strange, and it seemed unlikely that there should be another such in existence. Set at the opposite end of the mantelpiece from the lump of glass that had been dug from the sand, it looked like a creature from another world – freakish and fantastic as a harlequin. It seemed to be pirouetting through space; winking light like a fitful star. The contrast between the china so vivid and alert, and the glass so mute and contemplative, fascinated him, and wondering and amazed he asked himself how the two came to exist in the same world, let alone to stand upon the same narrow strip of marble in the same room. The question remained unanswered.

He now began to haunt the places which are most prolific of broken china, such as pieces of waste land between railway lines, sites of demolished houses, and commons in the neighbourhood of London. But china is seldom thrown from a great height; it is one of the rarest of human actions. You have to find in conjunction a very high house, and a woman of such reckless impulse and passionate prejudice that she flings her jar or pot straight from the window without thought of who is below. Broken china was to be found in plenty, but broken in some trifling domestic accident, without purpose or character. Nevertheless, he was often astonished, as he came to go into the question more deeply, by the immense variety of shapes to be found in London alone, and there was still more cause for wonder and speculation in the differences of qualities and designs. The finest specimens he would bring home and place upon his mantelpiece, where, however, their duty was more and more of an ornamental nature, since papers needing a weight to keep them down became scarcer and scarcer.

He neglected his duties, perhaps, or discharged them absent-mindedly, or his constituents when they visited him were unfavourably impressed by the appearance of his mantelpiece. At any rate he was not elected to represent them in Parliament, and his friend Charles, taking it much to heart and hurrying to condole with him, found him so little cast down by the disaster that he could only suppose that it was too serious a matter for him to realize all at once.

In truth, John had been that day to Barnes Common, and there under a furse bush had found a very remarkable piece of iron. It was almost identical with the glass in shape, massy and globular, but so cold and heavy, so black and metallic, that it was evidently alien to the earth and had its origin in one of the dead stars or was itself the cinder of a moon. It weighed his pocket down; it weighed the mantelpiece down; it radiated cold. And yet the meteorite stood upon the same ledge with the lump of glass and the star-shaped china.

As his eyes passed from one to another, the determination to possess objects that even surpassed these tormented the young man. He devoted himself more and more resolutely to the search. If he had not been consumed by ambition and convinced that one day some newly-discovered rubbish heap would reward him, the disappointments he had suffered, let alone the fatigue and derision, would have made him give up the pursuit. Provided with a bag and a long stick fitted with an adaptable hook, he ransacked all deposits of earth; raked beneath matted tangles of scrub; searched all alleys and spaces between walls where he had learned to expect to find objects of this kind thrown away. As his standard became higher and his taste more severe the disappointments were innumerable, but always some gleam of hope, some piece of china or glass curiously marked or broken, lured him on. Day after day passed. He was no longer young. His career – that is his political career – was a thing of the past. People gave up visiting him. He was too silent to be worth asking to dinner. He never talked to anyone about his serious ambitions; their lack of understanding was apparent in their behaviour.

He leaned back in his chair now and watched Charles lift the stones on the mantelpiece a dozen times and put them down emphatically to mark what he was saying about the conduct of the Government, without once noticing their existence.

'What was the truth of it, John?' asked Charles suddenly, turning and facing him. 'What made you give it up like that all in a second?'

'I've not given it up,' John replied.

'But you've not the ghost of a chance now,' said Charles roughly.

'I don't agree with you there,' said John with conviction. Charles looked at him and was profoundly uneasy; the most extraordinary doubts possessed him; he had a queer sense that they were talking about different things. He looked round to find some relief for his horrible depression, but the disorderly appearance of the room depressed him still further. What was that stick, and the old carpet bag hanging against the wall? And then those stones? Looking at John, something fixed and distant in his expression alarmed him. He knew only too well that his mere appearance upon a platform was out of the question.

'Pretty stones,' he said as cheerfully as he could; and saying that he had an appointment to keep, he left John – for ever.

In the Orchard

Miranda slept in the orchard, lying in a long chair beneath the apple-tree. Her book had fallen into the grass, and her finger still seemed to point at the sentence '*Ce pays est vraiment un des coins du monde où le rire des filles éclate le mieux* . . .'[1] as if she had fallen asleep just there. The opals on her finger flushed green, flushed rosy, and again flushed orange as the sun, oozing through the apple-trees, filled them. Then, when the breeze blew, her purple dress rippled like a flower attached to a stalk; the grasses nodded; and the white butterfly came blowing this way and that just above her face.

Four feet in the air over her head the apples hung. Suddenly there was a shrill clamour as if they were gongs of cracked brass beaten violently, irregularly, and brutally. It was only the school-children saying the multiplication table in unison, stopped by the teacher, scolded, and beginning to say the multiplication table over again. But this clamour passed four feet above Miranda's head, went through the apple boughs, and, striking against the cow-man's little boy who was picking blackberries in the hedge when he should have been at school, made him tear his thumb on the thorns.

Next there was a solitary cry – sad, human, brutal. Old Parsley was, indeed, blind drunk.

Then the very topmost leaves of the apple-tree, flat like little fish against the blue, thirty feet above the earth, chimed with a pensive and lugubrious note. It was the organ in the church playing one of Hymns Ancient and Modern.[2] The sound floated out and was cut into atoms by a flock of fieldfares[3] flying at an enormous speed – somewhere or other. Miranda lay asleep thirty feet beneath.

Then above the apple-tree and the pear-tree two hundred feet above Miranda lying asleep in the orchard bells thudded, intermittent, sullen, didactic, for six poor women of the parish were being churched[4] and the Rector was returning thanks to heaven.

And above that with a sharp squeak the golden feather of the church tower[5] turned from south to east. The wind changed. Above everything else it droned, above the woods, the meadows, the hills, miles above Miranda lying in the orchard asleep. It swept on, eyeless, brainless, meeting nothing that could stand against it, until, wheeling the other way, it turned south again. Miles below, in a space as big as the eye of a needle, Miranda stood upright and cried aloud: 'Oh, I shall be late for tea!'

Miranda slept in the orchard – or perhaps she was not asleep, for her lips moved very slightly as if they were saying, '*Ce pays est vraiment un des coins du monde . . . où le rire des filles . . . éclate . . . éclate . . . éclate . . .*' and then she smiled and let her body sink all its weight on to the enormous earth which rises, she thought, to carry me on its back as if I were a leaf, or a queen (here the children said the multiplication table), or, Miranda went on, I might be lying on the top of a cliff with the gulls screaming above me. The higher they fly, she continued, as the teacher scolded the children and rapped Jimmy over the knuckles till they bled, the deeper they look into the sea – into the sea, she repeated, and her fingers relaxed and her lips closed gently as if she were floating on the sea, and then, when the shout of the drunken man sounded overhead, she drew breath with an extraordinary ecstasy, for she thought that she heard life itself crying out from a rough tongue in a scarlet mouth, from the wind, from the bells, from the curved green leaves of the cabbages.

Naturally she was being married when the organ played the tune from Hymns Ancient and Modern, and, when the bells rang after the six poor women had been churched, the sullen intermittent thud made her think that the very earth shook with the hoofs of the horse that was galloping towards her ('Ah, I have only to wait!' she sighed), and it seemed to her that everything had already begun moving, crying, riding, flying round her, across her, towards her in a pattern.

Mary is chopping the wood, she thought; Pearman is herding the cows; the carts are coming up from the meadows; the rider – and she traced out the lines that the men, the carts, the birds, and the rider made over the countryside until they all seemed driven out, round, and across by the beat of her own heart.

Miles up in the air the wind changed; the golden feather of the church tower squeaked; and Miranda jumped up and cried: 'Oh, I shall be late for tea!'

Miranda slept in the orchard, or was she asleep or was she not asleep? Her purple dress stretched between the two apple-trees. There were twenty-four apple-trees in the orchard, some slanting slightly, others growing straight with a rush up the trunk which spread wide into branches and formed into round red or yellow drops. Each apple-tree had sufficient space. The sky exactly fitted the leaves. When the breeze blew, the line of the boughs against the wall slanted slightly and then returned. A wagtail flew diagonally from one corner to another. Cautiously hopping, a thrush advanced towards a fallen apple; from the other wall a sparrow fluttered just above the grass. The uprush of the trees was tied down by these movements; the whole was compacted by the orchard walls. For miles beneath the earth was clamped together; rippled on the surface with wavering air; and across the corner of the orchard the blue-green was slit by a purple streak. The wind changing, one bunch of apples was tossed so high that it blotted out two cows in the meadow ('Oh, I shall be late for tea!' cried Miranda), and the apples hung straight across the wall again.

A Woman's College from Outside

The feathering-white moon never let the sky grow dark; all night the chestnut blossoms were white in the green, and dim was the cow-parsley in the meadows.[1] Neither to Tartary nor to Arabia went the wind of the Cambridge courts, but lapsed dreamily in the midst of grey-blue clouds over the roofs of Newnham. There, in the garden, if she needed space to wander, she might find it among the trees; and as none but women's faces could meet her face, she might unveil it, blank, featureless, and gaze into rooms where at that hour, blank, featureless, eyelids white over eyes, ringless hands extended upon sheets, slept innumerable women. But here and there a light still burned.

A double light one might figure in Angela's room, seeing how bright Angela herself was, and how bright came back the reflection of herself from the square glass. The whole of her was perfectly delineated – perhaps the soul. For the glass held up an untrembling image – white and gold, red slippers, pale hair with blue stones in it, and never a ripple or shadow to break the smooth kiss of Angela and her reflection in the glass, as if she were glad to be Angela. Anyhow the moment was glad – the bright picture hung in the heart of night, the shrine hollowed in the nocturnal blackness. Strange indeed to have this visible proof of the rightness of things; this lily floating flawless[2] upon Time's pool, fearless, as if this were sufficient – this reflection. Which meditation she betrayed by turning, and the mirror held nothing at all, or only the brass bedstead, and she, running here and there, patting and darting, became like a woman in a house, and changed again, pursing her lips over a black book and marking with her finger what surely could not be a firm grasp of the science of economics. Only Angela Williams was at Newnham for the purpose of earning her living, and could not forget even in moments of impassioned adoration the cheques of her father at Swansea:[3] her mother washing in the scullery: pink frocks out to dry on the line; tokens that even the lily no longer floats flawless upon the pool, but has a name on a card like another.

A. Williams – one may read it in the moonlight; and next to it some Mary or Eleanor, Mildred, Sarah, Phoebe upon square cards on their doors. All names, nothing but names. The cool white light withered them and starched them until it seemed as if the only purpose of all these names was to rise martially in order should there be a call on them to extinguish a fire, suppress an insurrection, or pass an examination. Such is the power of names written upon cards pinned upon doors. Such too the resemblance, what with tiles, corridors, and bedroom doors, to dairy or nunnery, a place of seclusion or discipline, where the bowl of milk stands cool and pure and there's a great washing of linen.

At that very moment soft laughter came from behind a door. A prim-voiced clock struck the hour – one, two. Now if the clock were issuing his commands, they were disregarded. Fire, insurrection, examination, were all snowed under by laughter, or softly uprooted, the sound seeming to bubble up from the depths and gently waft away the hour, rules, discipline. The bed was strewn with cards. Sally was on the floor. Helena in the chair. Good Bertha clasping her hands by the fire-place. A. Williams came in yawning.

'Because it's utterly and intolerably damnable,' said Helena.

'Damnable,' echoed Bertha. Then yawned.

'We're not eunuchs.'

'I saw her slipping in by the back gate with that old hat on. They don't want us to know.'

'They?' said Angela. 'She.'

Then the laughter.

The cards were spread, falling with their red and yellow faces on the table, and hands were dabbled in the cards. Good Bertha, leaning with her head against the chair, sighed profoundly. For she would willingly have slept, but since night is free pasturage, a limitless field, since night is unmoulded richness, one must tunnel into its darkness. One must hang it with jewels. Night was shared in secret, day browsed on by the whole flock. The blinds were up. A mist was on the garden. Sitting on the floor by the window (while the others played), body, mind, both together, seemed blown through the air, to trail across the bushes. Ah, but she desired to stretch out in bed and to sleep! She believed that no one felt her desire for sleep; she believed humbly – sleepily – with sudden nods and lurchings, that other people were wide awake. When they laughed all together a bird chirped in its sleep out in the garden, as if the laughter –

Yes, as if the laughter (for she dozed now) floated out much like mists and attached itself by soft elastic shreds to plants and bushes, so that the garden was vaporous and clouded. And then, swept by the wind, the bushes would bow themselves and the white vapours blow off across the world.

From all the rooms where women slept this vapour issued, attaching itself to shrubs, like mist, and then blew freely out into the open. Elderly women slept, who would on waking immediately clasp the ivory rod of office. Now smooth and colourless, reposing deeply, they lay surrounded, lay supported, by the bodies of youth recumbent or grouped at the window; pouring forth into the garden this bubbling laughter, this irresponsible laughter: this laughter of mind and body floating away rules, hours, discipline: immensely fertilizing, yet formless, chaotic, trailing and straying and tufting the rose-bushes with shreds of vapour.

'Ah,' breathed Angela, standing at the window in her nightgown. Pain was in her voice. She leant her head out. The mist was cleft as if her voice parted it. She had been talking, while the others played, to Alice Avery, about Bamborough Castle;[4] the colour of the sands at evening; upon which Alice said she would write and settle the day, in August, and stooping, kissed her, at least touched her head with her hand, and Angela, positively unable to sit still, like one possessed of a wind-lashed sea in her heart, roamed up and down the room (the witness of such a scene) throwing her arms out to relieve this excitement, this astonishment at the incredible stooping of the miraculous tree with the golden fruit at its summit – hadn't it dropped into her arms? She held it glowing to her breast, a thing not to be touched, thought of, or spoken about, but left to glow there. And then, slowly putting there her stockings, there her slippers, folding her petticoat neatly on top, Angela, her other name being Williams, realized – how could she express it? – that after the dark churning of myriad ages here was light at the end of the tunnel; life; the world. Beneath her it lay – all good; all lovable. Such was her discovery.

Indeed, how could one then feel surprise if, lying in bed, she could not close her eyes? – something irresistibly unclosed them – if in the shallow darkness chair and chest of drawers looked stately, and the looking-glass precious with its ashen hint of day? Sucking her thumb like a child (her age nineteen last November), she lay in this good world, this new world, this world at the end of the tunnel, until a desire to see it or forestall it drove her, tossing her blankets, to guide herself to the window, and there, looking out upon the garden, where the mist lay, all the windows open, one fiery-bluish, something murmuring in the distance, the world of course, and the morning coming, 'Oh,' she cried, as if in pain.

The Lady in the Looking-Glass: A Reflection

People should not leave looking-glasses hanging in their rooms any more than they should leave open cheque books or letters confessing some hideous crime. One could not help looking, that summer afternoon, in the long glass that hung outside in the hall. Chance had so arranged it. From the depths of the sofa in the drawing-room one could see reflected in the Italian glass not only the marble-topped table opposite, but a stretch of the garden beyond. One could see a long grass path leading between banks of tall flowers until, slicing off an angle, the gold rim cut it off.

The house was empty, and one felt, since one was the only person in the drawing-room, like one of those naturalists who, covered with grass and leaves, lie watching the shyest animals – badgers, otters, kingfishers – moving about freely, themselves unseen. The room that afternoon was full of such shy creatures, lights and shadows, curtains blowing, petals falling – things that never happen, so it seems, if someone is looking. The quiet old country room with its rugs and stone chimney pieces, its sunken book-cases and red and gold lacquer cabinets, was full of such nocturnal creatures. They came pirouetting across the floor, stepping delicately with high-lifted feet and spread tails and pecking allusive beaks as if they had been cranes or flocks of elegant flamingoes whose pink was faded, or peacocks whose trains were veined with silver. And there were obscure flushes and darkenings too, as if a cuttlefish had suddenly suffused the air with purple; and the room had its passions and rages and envies and sorrows coming over it and clouding it, like a human being. Nothing stayed the same for two seconds together.

But, outside, the looking-glass reflected the hall table, the sunflowers, the garden path so accurately and so fixedly that they seemed held there in their reality unescapably. It was a strange contrast – all changing here, all stillness there. One could not help looking from one to the other. Meanwhile, since all the doors and windows were open in the heat, there was a perpetual sighing and ceasing sound, the voice of the transient and the perishing, it seemed, coming and going like human breath, while in the looking-glass things had ceased to breathe and lay still in the trance of immortality.

Half an hour ago the mistress of the house, Isabella Tyson, had gone down the grass path in her thin summer dress, carrying a basket, and had vanished, sliced off by the gilt rim of the looking-glass. She had gone presumably into the lower garden to pick flowers; or as it seemed more natural to suppose, to pick something light and fantastic and leafy and trailing, traveller's joy, or one of those elegant sprays of convolvulus that twine round ugly walls and burst here and there into white and violet blossoms. She suggested the fantastic and the tremulous convolvulus rather than the upright aster, the starched zinnia, or her own burning roses alight like lamps on the straight posts of their rose trees. The comparison showed how very little, after all these years, one knew about her; for it is impossible that any woman of flesh and blood of fifty-five or sixty should be really a wreath or a tendril. Such comparisons are worse than idle and superficial – they are cruel even, for they come like the convolvulus itself trembling between one's eyes and the truth. There must be truth; there must be a wall. Yet it was strange that after knowing her all these years one could not say what the truth about Isabella was; one still made up phrases like this about convolvulus and traveller's joy. As for facts, it was a fact that she was a spinster; that she was rich; that she had bought this house and collected with her own hands – often in the most obscure corners of the world and at great risk from poisonous stings and Oriental diseases – the rugs, the chairs, the cabinets which now lived their nocturnal life before one's eyes. Sometimes it seemed as if they knew more about her than we, who sat on them, wrote at them, and trod on them so carefully, were allowed to know. In each of these cabinets were many little drawers, and each almost certainly held letters, tied with bows of ribbon, sprinkled with sticks of lavender or rose leaves. For it was another fact – if facts were what one wanted – that Isabella had known many people, had had many friends; and thus if one had the audacity to open a drawer and read her letters, one would find the traces of many agitations, of appointments to meet, of upbraidings for not having met, long letters of intimacy and affection, violent letters of jealousy and reproach, terrible final words of parting – for all those interviews and assignations had led to nothing – that is, she had never married, and yet, judging from the mask-like indifference of her face, she had gone through twenty times more of passion and experience than those whose loves are trumpeted forth for all the world to hear. Under the stress of thinking about Isabella, her room became more shadowy and symbolic; the corners seemed darker, the legs of chairs and tables more spindly and hieroglyphic.

Suddenly these reflections were ended violently and yet without a sound. A large black form loomed into the looking-glass; blotted out everything, strewed the table with a packet of marble tablets veined with pink and grey, and was gone. But the picture was entirely altered. For the moment it was unrecognisable and irrational and entirely out of focus. One could not relate these tablets to any human purpose. And then by degrees some logical process set to work on them and began ordering and arranging them and bringing them into the fold of common experience. One realised at last that they were merely letters. The man had brought the post.

There they lay on the marble-topped table, all dripping with light and colour at first and crude and unabsorbed. And then it was strange to see how they were drawn in and arranged and composed and made part of the picture and granted that stillness and immortality which the looking-glass conferred. They lay there invested with a new reality and significance and with a greater heaviness, too, as if it would have needed a chisel to dislodge them from the table. And, whether it was fancy or not, they seemed to have become not merely a handful of casual letters but to be tablets graven with eternal truth – if one could read them, one would know everything there was to be known about Isabella, yes, and about life, too. The pages inside those marble-looking envelopes must be cut deep and scored thick with meaning. Isabella would come in, and take them, one by one, very slowly, and open them, and read them carefully word by word, and then with a profound sigh of comprehension, as if she had seen to the bottom of everything, she would tear the envelopes to little bits and tie the letters together and lock the cabinet drawer in her determination to conceal what she did not wish to be known.

The thought served as a challenge. Isabella did not wish to be known – but she should no longer escape. It was absurd, it was monstrous. If she concealed so much and knew so much one must prize her open with the first tool that came to hand – the imagination. One must fix one's mind upon her at that very moment. One must fasten her down there. One must refuse to be put off any longer with sayings and doings such as the moment brought forth – with dinners and visits and polite conversations. One must put oneself in her shoes. If one took the phrase literally, it was easy to see the shoes in which she stood, down in the lower garden, at this moment. They were very narrow and long and fashionable – they were made of the softest and most flexible leather. Like everything she wore, they were exquisite. And she would be standing under the high hedge in the lower part of the garden, raising the scissors that were tied to her waist to cut some dead flower, some overgrown branch. The sun would beat down on her face, into her eyes; but no, at the critical moment a veil of cloud covered the sun, making the expression of her eyes doubtful – was it mocking or tender, brilliant or dull? One could only see the indeterminate outline of her rather faded, fine face looking at the sky. She was thinking, perhaps, that she must order a new net for the strawberries; that she must send flowers to Johnson's widow; that it was time she drove over to see the Hippesleys in their new house. Those were the things she talked about at dinner certainly. But one was tired of the things that she talked about at dinner. It was her profounder state of being that one wanted to catch and turn to words, the state that is to the mind what breathing is to the body, what one calls happiness or unhappiness. At the mention of those words it became obvious, surely, that she must be happy. She was rich; she was distinguished; she had many friends; she travelled – she bought rugs in Turkey and blue pots in Persia. Avenues of pleasure radiated this way and that from where she stood with her scissors raised to cut the trembling branches while the lacy clouds veiled her face.

Here with a quick movement of her scissors she snipped the spray of traveller's joy and it fell to the ground. As it fell, surely some light came in too, surely one could penetrate a little farther into her being. Her mind then was filled with tenderness and regret . . . To cut an overgrown branch saddened her because it had once lived, and life was dear to her. Yes, and at the same time the fall of the branch would suggest to her how she must die herself and all the futility and evanescence of things. And then again quickly catching this thought up, with her instant good sense, she thought life had treated her well; even if fall she must, it was to lie on the earth and moulder sweetly into the roots of violets. So she stood thinking. Without making any thought precise – for she was one of those reticent people whose minds hold their thoughts enmeshed in clouds of silence – she was filled with thoughts. Her mind was like her room, in which lights advanced and retreated, came pirouetting and stepping delicately, spread their tails, pecked their way; and then her whole being was suffused, like the room again, with a cloud of some profound knowledge, some unspoken regret, and then she was full of locked drawers, stuffed with letters, like her cabinets. To talk of 'prizing her open' as if she were an oyster, to use any but the finest and subtlest and most pliable tools upon her was impious and absurd. One must imagine – here was she in the looking-glass. It made one start.

She was so far off at first that one could not see her clearly. She came lingering and pausing, here straightening a rose, there lifting a pink to smell it, but she never stopped; and all the time she became larger and larger in the looking-glass, more and more completely the person into whose mind one had been trying to penetrate. One verified her by degrees – fitted the qualities one had discovered into this visible body. There were her grey-green dress, and her long shoes, her basket, and something sparkling at her throat. She came so gradually that she did not seem to derange the pattern in the glass, but only to bring in some new element which gently moved and altered the other objects as if asking them, courteously, to make room for her. And the letters and the table and the grass walk and the sunflowers which had been waiting in the looking-glass separated and opened out so that she might be received among them. At last there she was, in the hall. She stopped dead. She stood by the table. She stood perfectly still. At once the looking-glass began to pour over her a light that seemed to fix her; that seemed like some acid to bite off the unessential and superficial and to leave only the truth. It was an enthralling spectacle. Everything dropped from her – clouds, dress, basket, diamond – all that one had called the creeper and convolvulus. Here was the hard wall beneath. Here was the woman herself. She stood naked in that pitiless light. And there was nothing. Isabella was perfectly empty. She had no thoughts. She had no friends. She cared for nobody. As for her letters, they were all bills. Look, as she stood there, old and angular, veined and lined, with her high nose and her wrinkled neck, she did not even trouble to open them.

People should not leave looking-glasses hanging in their rooms.

The Shooting Party

I

She got in and put her suitcase on the rack, and the brace of pheasants on top of it. Then she sat down in the corner. The train was rattling through the Midlands, and the fog, which came in when she opened the door, seemed to enlarge the carriage and set the four travellers apart. Obviously M. M. – those were the initials on the suitcase – had been staying the week-end with a shooting party – obviously, for she was telling over the story now, lying back in her corner. She did not shut her eyes. But clearly she did not see the man opposite, nor the coloured photograph of York Minster.[1] She must have heard, too, what they had been saying. For as she gazed, her lips moved; now and then she smiled. And she was handsome; a cabbage rose; a russet apple; tawny; but scarred on the jaw – the scar lengthened when she smiled. Since she was telling over the story she must have been a guest there, and yet, dressed as she was, out of fashion, as women dressed years ago in pictures in fashion plates of sporting newspapers, she did not seem exactly a guest, nor yet a maid. Had she had a basket with her she would have been the woman who breeds fox-terriers; the owner of the Siamese cat; someone connected with hounds and horses. But she had only a suitcase and the pheasants. Somehow, therefore, she must have wormed her way into the room that she was seeing through the stuffing of the carriage, and the man's bald head, and the picture of York Minster. And she must have listened to what they were saying, for now, like somebody imitating the noise that someone else makes, she made a little click at the back of her throat: 'Chk,' 'Chk.' Then she smiled.

II

'Chk' said Miss Antonia, pinching her glasses on her nose. The damp leaves fell across the long windows of the gallery; one or two stuck, fish-shaped, and lay like inlaid brown wood upon the window panes. Then the trees in the Park shivered, and the leaves, flaunting down, seemed to make the shiver visible – the damp brown shiver.

'Chk' Miss Antonia sniffed again, and pecked at the flimsy white stuff that she held in her hands, as a hen pecks nervously, rapidly at a piece of white bread.

The wind sighed. The room was draughty. The doors did not fit, nor the windows. Now and then a ripple, like a reptile, ran under the carpet. On the carpet lay panels of green and yellow, when the sun rested, and then the sun moved and pointed a finger as if in mockery at a hole in the carpet; and stopped. And then on it went, the sun's feeble but impartial finger, and lay upon the coat of arms over the fireplace – gently illumined the shield; the pendant grapes; the mermaid, and the spears. Miss Antonia looked up as the light strengthened. Vast lands, so they said, the old people had owned – her forefathers, the Rashleighs. Over there. Up the Amazons. Freebooters. Voyagers. Sacks of emeralds. Nosing round the islands. Taking captives. Maidens. There she was, all scales from the tail to the waist. Miss Antonia grinned. Down struck the finger of the sun and her eye went with it. Now it rested on a silver frame; on a photograph; on an egg-shaped baldish head; on a lip that stuck out under the moustache; and the name 'Edward' written with a flourish beneath.[2]

'The King . . .' Miss Antonia muttered, turning the film of white upon her knee, 'had the blue room,' she added with a toss of her head. The light faded.

Out in the King's Ride the pheasants were being driven across the noses of the guns. Up they spurted from the underwood like heavy rockets, reddish-purple rockets, and as they rose the guns cracked in order, eagerly, sharply, as if a line of dogs had suddenly barked.

In the deep-cut road beneath the hanger[3] a cart stood, laid already with soft warm bodies, with limp claws and still lustrous eyes. The birds seemed alive still, but swooning under their rich damp feathers. They looked relaxed and comfortable, stirring slightly, as if they slept upon a warm bank of soft feathers on the floor of the cart.

Then the Squire, with the hang-dog purple-stained face, in the shabby gaiters, cursed and raised his gun.

Miss Antonia stitched on. Now and then a tongue of flame reached round the grey log that stretched from one bar to another across the grate; ate it greedily, then died out, leaving a white bracelet where the bark had been eaten off.

Now, silently, the enormously high door opened. Two lean men came in, and drew a table over the hole in the carpet. They went out; they came in. They laid a cloth upon the table. They went out: they came in. They brought a green baize basket of knives and forks; and glasses; and sugar casters; and salt cellars; and bread; and a silver vase with three chrysanthemums in it. And the table was laid. Miss Antonia stitched on.

Again the door opened, pushed feebly this time. A little dog trotted in, a spaniel, nosing nimbly; it paused. The door stood open. And then, leaning on her stick, heavily, old Miss Rashleigh entered.[4] A white shawl, diamond fastened, clouded her baldness. Miss Antonia went on stitching.

'Shooting,' she said at last.

Old Miss Rashleigh nodded. 'In the King's Ride,' she said. She gripped her stick. They sat waiting.

The shooters had moved now from the King's Ride to the Home Woods. They stood in the purple ploughed field outside. But above the mist and the smoke was an island of blue – faint blue, pure blue – alone in the sky. And in the innocent air, as if straying alone like a cherub, a bell from a far hidden steeple frolicked, gambolled, then faded. Then again up shot the rockets, the reddish-purple pheasants. Up and up they went. Again the guns barked; the smoke balls formed; loosened, dispersed. And the warm damp bodies, still languid and soft, as if in a swoon, were bunched together by men in gaiters and flung into the cart.

'There!' grunted Milly Masters, the housekeeper, throwing down her glasses. She was stitching too in the small dark room that overlooked the stable yard. The jersey, the rough woollen jersey, for her son, the boy who cleaned the church, was finished. 'The end o' that,' she muttered. The she heard the cart. Up she got. With her hands to her hair, she stood in the yard, in the wind.

'Coming!' she laughed, and the scar on her cheek lengthened. She unbolted the door of the game-room as Wing, the keeper, drove the cart over the cobbles. The birds were dead now, their claws gripped tight, though they gripped nothing. The leathery eyelids were creased greyly over their eyes. Mrs. Masters the housekeeper, Wing the gamekeeper, took bunches of dead birds by the neck and flung them down on the slate floor of the game-larder. Then Wing lifted the tail of the cart and drove in the pins which secured it. The sides of the cart were stuck about with little grey-blue feathers and the floor was smeared and stained with blood. But it was empty.

'The last of the lot!' Milly Masters grinned as the cart drove off.

'Luncheon is served, ma'am,' said the butler. He pointed at the table; he directed the footman. The dish with the silver cover was placed precisely there where he pointed.

Miss Antonia laid her white film upon the basket; put away her silk; her thimble; stuck her needle through a piece of flannel; and hung her glasses on a hook upon her breast. Then she rose.

'Luncheon!' she barked in old Miss Rashleigh's ear. One second later old Miss Rashleigh stretched her leg out; gripped her stick; and rose too. Both old women advanced slowly to the table; and were tucked in by the butler and the footman, one at this end, one at that. Off came the silver cover. And there was the pheasant, featherless, gleaming; the thighs tightly pressed to its side; and little mounds of breadcrumbs were heaped at either end.

Miss Antonia drew the carving knife across the pheasant's breast firmly. She cut two slices and laid them on a plate. Deftly the footman whipped it from her, and old Miss Rashleigh raised her knife. Shots rang out in the wood under the window.

'Coming?' said old Miss Rashleigh, suspending her fork.

She took a mouthful of pheasant.

'In the Home Wood now,' said Miss Antonia. 'Hugh's last shoot.' She drew her knife down the other side of the breast. She added potatoes and gravy, brussels sprouts and bread sauce methodically in a circle round the slices on her plate. The old ladies ate quietly; silently; nor did they hurry themselves; methodically they cleaned the bird. Bones only were left on their plates. Then the butler drew the decanter towards Miss Antonia, and paused for a moment with his head bent.

'Give it here, Griffiths,' said Miss Antonia, and took the carcass in her fingers and tossed it to the spaniel beneath the table.

'Coming closer,' said Miss Rashleigh, listening. The wind was rising.

'Birds wild,' Miss Antonia nodded, watching the helter skelter.

As they sipped their eyes became lustrous like half-precious stones held to the light. Slate blue were Miss Rashleigh's; Miss Antonia's red, like port. And their laces and their flounces seemed to quiver, as if their bodies were warm and languid underneath their feathers as they drank.

'It was a day like this, d'you remember?' said old Miss Rashleigh, fingering her glass. 'They brought him home . . . a bullet through his heart. A bramble, so they said. Tripped. Caught his foot . . .' She chuckled as she sipped her wine.

'And John . . .' said Miss Antonia. 'The mare, they said, put her foot in a hole. Died in the field. The hunt rode over him. He came home, too, on a shutter . . .' They sipped again.

'Remember Lily?' said old Miss Rashleigh. 'A bad 'un.' She shook her head. 'Riding with a scarlet tassel on her cane . . .'

'Rotten at the heart!' cried Miss Antonia. 'Remember the Colonel's letter? "Your son rode as if he had twenty devils in him – charged at the head of his men!" Then one white devil – ah hah!' she sipped again.

'The men of our house,' began Miss Rashleigh. She raised her glass. She held it high, as if she toasted the mermaid carved in plaster on the fireplace. She paused. The guns were barking. Something cracked in the woodwork. Or was it a rat running behind the plaster?

'Always women . . .' Miss Antonia nodded. 'The men of our house. Pink and white Lucy at the Mill – d'you remember?'

'Ellen's daughter at the Goat and Sickle,' Miss Rashleigh added.

'And the girl at the tailor's,' Miss Antonia murmured, 'where Hugh bought his riding breeches, the little dark shop on the right . . .'

'– That used to be flooded every winter. It's *his* boy,' Miss Antonia chuckled, leaning towards her sister, 'that cleans the church.'

There was a crash. A slate had fallen down the chimney. The great log had snapped in two. Flakes of plaster fell from the shield above the fireplace.

'Falling,' old Miss Rashleigh chuckled. 'Falling.'

'And who,' said Miss Antonia, looking at the flakes on the carpet, 'who's to pay?'

Crowing like old babies, indifferent, reckless, they laughed, crossed to the fireplace, and sipped their sherry by the wood ashes and the plaster, until each glass held only one drop of wine, reddish purple, at the bottom. And this the old women did not wish to part with, so it seemed; for they fingered their glasses, as they sat side by side by the ashes; but they never raised them to their lips.

'Milly Masters in the still-room,' began old Miss Rashleigh. 'She's our brother's . . .'

A shot barked beneath the window. It cut the string that held the rain. Down it poured, down, down, down, in straight rods, whipping the windows. Light faded from the carpet. Light faded in their eyes too, as they sat by the white ashes listening. Their eyes became like pebbles, taken from water; grey stones dulled and dried. And their hands gripped their hands like the claws of dead birds gripping nothing. And they shrivelled as if the bodies inside the clothes had shrunk. Then Miss Antonia raised her glass to the mermaid. It was the last toast; the last drop; she drank it off. 'Coming!' she croaked, and slapped the glass down. A door banged below. Then another. Then another. Feet could be heard trampling, yet shuffling, along the corridor towards the gallery.

'Closer! Closer!' grinned Miss Rashleigh, baring her three yellow teeth.

The immensely high door burst open. In rushed three great hounds and stood panting. Then there entered, slouching, the Squire himself in shabby gaiters. The dogs pressed round him, tossing their heads, snuffling at his pockets. Then they bounded forward. They smelt the meat. The floor of the gallery waved like a wind-lashed forest with the tails and backs of the great questing hounds. They snuffed the table. They pawed the cloth. Then with a wild neighing whimper they flung themselves upon the yellow spaniel who was gnawing the carcass under the table.

'Curse you, curse you!' howled the Squire. But his voice was weak, as if he shouted against a wind. 'Curse you, curse you!' he shouted, now cursing his sisters.

Miss Antonia and Miss Rashleigh rose to their feet. The great dogs had seized the spaniel. They worried him, they mauled him with their great yellow teeth. The Squire swung a leather knotted tawse this way, that way, cursing the dogs, cursing his sisters, in the voice that sounded so loud yet was so weak. With one lash he curled to the ground the vase of chrysanthemums. Another caught old Miss Rashleigh on the cheek. The old woman staggered backwards. She fell against the mantelpiece. Her stick, striking wildly, struck the shield above the fireplace. She fell with a thud upon the ashes. The shield of the Rashleighs crashed from the wall. Under the mermaid, under the spears, she lay buried.

The wind lashed the panes of the glass; shots volleyed in the Park and a tree fell. And then King Edward in the silver frame slid, toppled and fell too.

III

The grey mist had thickened in the carriage. It hung down like a veil; it seemed to put the four travellers in the corners at a great distance from each other, though in fact they were as close as the walls of a third-class railway carriage could bring them. The effect was strange. The handsome if elderly, the well-dressed if rather shabby woman who had got into the train at some station in the Midlands seemed to have lost her shape. Her body had become all mist. Only her eyes gleamed, changed, lived all by themselves, it seemed; eyes without a body; blue-grey eyes seeing something invisible. In the misty air they shone out, they moved, so that in the sepulchral atmosphere – the windows were blurred, the lamps haloed with fog – they were like lights dancing, will o' the wisps that move, people say, over the graves of unquiet sleepers in churchyards. An absurd idea! Mere fancy! Yet, after all, since there is nothing that does not leave some residue, and memory is a light that dances in the mind when the reality is buried, why should not the eyes there, gleaming, moving, be the ghost of a family, of an age, of a civilisation dancing over the grave?

The train slowed down. One after another, lamps stood up; held their yellow heads erect for a second; then were felled. Up they stood again as the train slid into the station. The lights massed and blazed. And the eyes in the corner? They were shut; the lids were closed. They saw nothing. Perhaps the light was too strong. And, of course, in the full blaze of the station lamps it was plain – she was quite an ordinary, rather elderly woman travelling to London on some quite ordinary piece of business –

something connected with a cat or a horse or a dog. She reached for her suitcase, rose, and took the pheasants from the rack. But did she, all the same, as she opened the carriage door and stepped out, murmur 'Chk, Chk,' as she passed?

The Duchess and the Jeweller

Oliver Bacon lived at the top of a house overlooking the Green Park.[1] He had a flat; chairs jutted out at the right angles – chairs covered in hide. Sofas filled the bays of the windows – sofas covered in tapestry. The windows, the three long windows, had the proper allowance of discreet net and figured satin. The mahogany sideboard bulged discreetly with the right brandies, whiskeys and liqueurs. And from the middle window he looked down upon the glossy roofs of fashionable cars packed in the narrow straits of Piccadilly. A more central position could not be imagined. And at eight in the morning he would have his breakfast brought in on a tray by a manservant; the manservant would unfold his crimson dressing-gown; he would rip his letters open with his long pointed nails and would extract thick white cards of invitation upon which the engraving stood up roughly from duchesses, countesses, viscountesses and Honourable Ladies. Then he would wash; then he would eat his toast; then he would read his paper by the bright burning fire of electric coals.

'Behold Oliver,' he would say, addressing himself. 'You who began life in a filthy little alley, you who . . .' and he would look down at his legs, so shapely in their perfect trousers; at his boots; at his spats. They were all shaped, shining; cut from the best cloth by the best scissors in Savile Row.[2] But he dismantled himself often and became again a little boy in a dark alley. He had once thought that the height of his ambition – selling stolen dogs to fashionable women in Whitechapel. And once he had been done.[3] 'Oh, Oliver,' his mother had wailed. 'Oh, Oliver! When will you have sense, my son?' . . . Then he had gone behind a counter; had sold cheap watches; then he had taken a wallet to Amsterdam . . . At that memory he would chuckle – the old Oliver remembering the young. Yes, he had done well with the three diamonds; also there was the commission on the emerald. After that he went into the private room behind the shop in Hatton Garden;[4] the room with the scales, the safe, the thick magnifying glasses. And then . . . and then . . . He chuckled. When he passed through the knots of jewellers in the hot evening who were discussing prices, gold mines, diamonds, reports from South Africa, one of them would lay a finger to the side of his nose and murmur, 'Hum–m–m,' as he passed. It was no more than a murmur; no more than a nudge on the shoulder, a finger on the nose, a buzz that ran through the cluster of jewellers in Hatton Garden on a hot afternoon – oh, many years ago now! But still Oliver felt it purring down his spine, the nudge, the murmur that meant, 'Look at him – young Oliver, the young jeweller – there he goes.' Young he was then. And he dressed better and better; and had, first a hansom cab; then a car; and first he went up to the dress circle, then down into the stalls. And he had a villa at Richmond,[5] overlooking thc river, with trellises of red roses; and Mademoiselle used to pick one every morning and stick it in his buttonhole.

'So,' said Oliver Bacon, rising and stretching his legs. 'So . . . '

And he stood beneath the picture of an old lady on the mantelpiece and raised his hands. 'I have kept my word,' he said, laying his hands together, palm to palm, as if he were doing homage to her. 'I have won my bet.' That was so; he was the richest jeweller in England; but his nose, which was long and flexible, like an elephant's trunk, seemed to say by its curious quiver at the nostrils (but it seemed as if the whole nose quivered, not only the nostrils) that he was not satisfied yet; still smelt something under the ground a little further off. Imagine a giant hog in a pasture rich with truffles; after unearthing this truffle and that, still it smells a bigger, a blacker truffle under the ground further off. So Oliver snuffed always in the rich earth of Mayfair another truffle, a blacker, a bigger further off.

Now then he straightened the pearl in his tie, cased himself in his smart blue overcoat; took his yellow gloves and his cane; and swayed as he descended the stairs and half snuffed, half sighed through his long sharp nose as he passed out into Piccadilly. For was he not still a sad man, a dissatisfied man, a man who seeks something that is hidden, though he had won his bet?

He swayed slightly as he walked, as the camel at the zoo sways from side to side when it walks along the asphalt paths laden with grocers and their wives eating from paper bags and throwing little bits of silver paper crumpled up on to the path. The camel despises the grocers; the camel is dissatisfied with its lot; the camel sees the blue lake and the fringe of palm trees in front of it. So the great jeweller, the greatest jeweller in the whole world, swung down Piccadilly, perfectly dressed, with his gloves, with his cane; but dissatisfied still, till he reached the dark little shop, that was famous in France, in Germany, in Austria, in Italy, and all over America – the dark little shop in the street off Bond Street.[6]

As usual he strode through the shop without speaking, though the four men, the two old men, Marshall and Spencer, and the two young men, Hammond and Wicks, stood straight behind the counter as he passed and looked at him, envying him. It was only with one finger of the amber-coloured glove, waggling, that he acknowledged their presence. And he went in and shut the door of his private room behind him.

Then he unlocked the grating that barred the window. The cries of Bond Street came in; the purr of the distant traffic. The light from reflectors at the back of the shop struck upwards. One tree waved six green leaves, for it was June. But Mademoiselle had married Mr Pedder of the local brewery – no one stuck roses in his buttonhole now.

'So,' he half sighed, half snorted, 'so . . .'

Then he touched a spring in the wall and slowly the panelling slid open, and behind it were the steel safes, five, no, six of them, all of burnished steel. He twisted a key; unlocked one; then another. Each was lined with a pad of deep crimson velvet; in each lay jewels – bracelets, necklaces, rings, tiaras, ducal coronets; loose stones in glass shells; rubies, emeralds, pearls, diamonds. All safe, shining, cool, yet burning, eternally, with their own compressed light.

'Tears!' said Oliver, looking at the pearls.

'Heart's blood!' he said, looking at the rubies.

'Gunpowder!' he continued, rattling the diamonds so that they flashed and blazed.

'Gunpowder enough to blow up Mayfair – sky high, high, high!' He threw his head back and made a sound like a horse neighing as he said it.

The telephone buzzed obsequiously in a low muted voice on his table. He shut the safe.

'In ten minutes,' he said. 'Not before.' And he sat down at his desk and looked at the heads of the Roman emperors that were graved on his sleeve links. And again he dismantled himself and became once more the little boy playing marbles in the alley where they sell stolen dogs on Sunday. He became that wily astute little boy, with lips like wet cherries. He dabbled his fingers in ropes of tripe; he dipped them in pans of frying fish; he dodged in and out among the crowds. He was slim, lissome, with eyes like licked stones. And now – now – the hands of the clock ticked on. One, two, three, four . . . The Duchess of Lambourne waited his pleasure; the Duchess of Lambourne, daughter of a hundred Earls. She would wait for ten minutes on a chair at the counter. She would wait his pleasure. She would wait till he was ready to see her. He watched the clock in its shagreen[7] case. The hand moved on. With each tick the clock handed him – so it seemed – pâté de foie gras; a glass of champagne; another of fine brandy; a cigar costing one guinea. The clock laid them on the table beside him, as the ten minutes passed. Then he heard soft slow footsteps approaching; a rustle in the corridor. The door opened. Mr Hammond flattened himself against the wall.

'Her Grace!' he announced.

And he waited there, flattened against the wall.

And Oliver, rising, could hear the rustle of the dress of the Duchess as she came down the passage. Then she loomed up, filling the door, filling the room with the aroma, the prestige, the arrogance, the pomp, the pride of all the Dukes and Duchesses swollen in one wave. And as a wave breaks, she broke, as she sat down, spreading and splashing and falling over Oliver Bacon the great jeweller, covering him with sparkling bright colours, green, rose, violet; and odours; and iridescences; and rays shooting from fingers, nodding from plumes, flashing from silk; for she was very large, very fat, tightly girt in pink taffeta, and past her prime. As a parasol with many flounces, as a peacock with many feathers, shuts its flounces, folds it feathers, so she subsided and shut herself as she sank down in the leather armchair.

'Good morning, Mr Bacon,' said the Duchess. And she held out her hand which came through the slit of her white glove. And Oliver bent low as he shook it. And as their hands touched the link was forged between them once more. They were friends, yet enemies; he was master, she was mistress; each cheated the other, each needed the other, each feared the other, each felt this and knew this every time they touched hands thus in the little back room with the white light outside, and the tree with its six leaves, and the sound of the street in the distance and behind them the safes.

'And today, Duchess – what can I do for you today?' said Oliver, very softly.

The Duchess opened; her heart, her private heart, gaped wide. And with a sigh, but no words, she took from her bag a long wash-leather pouch – it looked like a lean yellow ferret. And from a slit in the ferret's belly she dropped pearls – ten pearls. They rolled from the slit in the ferret's belly – one, two, three, four – like the eggs of some heavenly bird.

'All that's left me, dear Mr Bacon,' she moaned. Five, six, seven – down they rolled, down the slopes of the vast mountain sides that fell between her knees into one narrow valley – the eighth, the ninth, and the tenth. There they lay in the glow of the peach-blossom taffeta. Ten pearls.

'From the Appleby cincture,'[8] she mourned. 'The last . . . the last of them all.'

Oliver stretched out and took one of the pearls between finger and thumb. It was round, it was lustrous. But real was it, or false? Was she lying again? Did she dare?

She laid her plump padded finger across her lips. 'If the Duke knew . . .' she whispered. 'Dear Mr Bacon, a bit of bad luck . . .'

Been gambling again, had she?

'That villain! That sharper!' she hissed.

The man with the chipped cheek bone? A bad 'un. And the Duke was straight as a poker; with side whiskers; would cut her off, shut her up down there if he knew – what I know, thought Oliver, and glanced at the safe.

'Araminta, Daphne, Diana,' she moaned. 'It's for *them*.'

The Ladies Araminta, Daphne, Diana – her daughters. He knew them; adored them. But it was Diana he loved.

'You have all my secrets,' she leered. Tears slid; tears fell; tears, like diamonds, collecting powder in the ruts of her cherry-blossom cheeks.

'Old friend,' she murmured, 'old friend.'

'Old friend,' he repeated, 'old friend,' as if he licked the words.

'How much?' he queried.

She covered the pearls with her hand.

'Twenty thousand,' she whispered.

But was it real or false, the one he held in his hand? The Appleby cincture – hadn't she sold it already? He would ring for Spencer or Hammond. 'Take it and test it,' he would say. He stretched to the bell.

'You will come down tomorrow?' she urged, she interrupted. 'The Prime Minister – His Royal Highness . . .' She stopped. 'And Diana,' she added.

Oliver took his hand off the bell.

He looked past her, at the backs of the houses in Bond Street. But he saw, not the houses in Bond Street, but a dimpling river; and trout rising and salmon; and the Prime Minister; and himself too; in white waistcoats; and then, Diana. He looked down at the pearl in his hand. But how could he test it, in the light of the river, in the light of the eyes of Diana? But the eyes of the Duchess were on him.

'Twenty thousand,' she moaned. 'My honour!'

The honour of the mother of Diana! He drew his cheque book towards him; he took out his pen.

'Twenty,' he wrote. Then he stopped writing. The eyes of the old woman in the picture were on him – of the old woman, his mother.

'Oliver!' she warned him. 'Have sense? Don't be a fool!'

'Oliver!' the Duchess entreated – it was 'Oliver' now, not 'Mr Bacon'. 'You'll come for a long week-end?'

Alone in the woods with Diana! Riding alone in the woods with Diana!

'Thousand,' he wrote, and signed it.

'Here you are,' he said.

And there opened all the flounces of the parasol, all the plumes of the peacock, the radiance of the wave, the swords and spears of Agincourt, as she rose from her chair. And the two old men and the two young men, Spencer and Marshall, Wicks and Hammond, flattened themselves behind the counter envying him as he led her through the shop to the door. And he waggled his yellow glove in their faces, and she held her honour – a cheque for twenty thousand pounds with his signature – quite firmly in her hands.

'Are they false or are they real?' asked Oliver, shutting his private door. There they were, ten pearls on the blotting paper on the table. He took them to the window. He held them under his lens to the light . . . This, then, was the truffle he had routed out of the earth! Rotten at the centre – rotten at the core!

'Forgive me, oh my mother!' he sighed, raising his hands as if he asked pardon of the old woman in the picture. And again he was a little boy in the alley where they sold dogs on Sunday.

'For,' he murmured, laying the palms of his hands together, 'it is to be a long week-end.'

Lappin and Lapinova

They were married. The wedding march pealed out. The pigeons fluttered. Small boys in Eton jackets[1] threw rice; a fox-terrier sauntered across the path; and Ernest Thorburn led his bride to the car through that small inquisitive crowd of complete strangers which always collects in London to enjoy other people's happiness or unhappiness. Certainly he looked handsome and she looked shy. More rice was thrown, and the car moved off.

That was on Tuesday. Now it was Saturday. Rosalind had still to get used to the fact that she was Mrs. Ernest Thorburn. Perhaps she never would get used to the fact that she was Mrs. Ernest Anybody, she thought, as she sat in the bow window of the hotel looking over the lake to the mountains,[2] and waited for her husband to come down to breakfast. Ernest was a difficult name to get used to. It was not the name she would have chosen. She would have preferred Timothy, Antony, or Peter. He did not look like Ernest either. The name suggested the Albert Memorial, mahogany sideboards, steel engravings of the Prince Consort with his family – her mother-in-law's dining-room in Porchester Terrace[3] in short.

But here he was. Thank goodness he did not look like Ernest – no. But what did he look like? She glanced at him sideways. Well, when he was eating toast he looked like a rabbit. Not that anyone else would have seen a likeness to a creature so diminutive and timid in this spruce, muscular young man with the straight nose, the blue eyes, and the very firm mouth. But that made it all the more amusing. His nose twitched very slightly when he ate. So did her pet rabbit's. She kept watching his nose twitch; and then she had to explain, when he caught her looking at him, why she laughed.

'It's because you're like a rabbit, Ernest,' she said. 'Like a wild rabbit,' she added, looking at him. 'A hunting rabbit; a King Rabbit; a rabbit that makes laws for all the other rabbits.'

Ernest had no objection to being that kind of rabbit, and since it amused her to see him twitch his nose – he had never known that his nose twitched – he twitched it on purpose. And she laughed and laughed; and he laughed too, so that the maiden ladies and the fishing man and the Swiss waiter in his greasy black jacket all guessed right; they were very happy. But how long does such happiness last? they asked themselves; and each answered according to his own circumstances.

At lunch time, seated on a clump of heather beside the lake, 'Lettuce, rabbit?' said Rosalind, holding out the lettuce that had been provided to eat with the hard-boiled eggs. 'Come and take it out of my hand,' she added, and he stretched out and nibbled the lettuce and twitched his nose.

'Good rabbit, nice rabbit,' she said, patting him, as she used to pat her tame rabbit at home. But that was absurd. He was not a tame rabbit, whatever he was. She turned it into French. 'Lapin,' she called him. But whatever he was, he was not a French rabbit. He was simply and solely English – born in Porchester Terrace, educated at Rugby;[4] now a clerk in His Majesty's Civil Service. So she tried 'Bunny' next; but that was worse. 'Bunny' was someone plump and soft and comic; he was thin and hard and serious. Still, his nose twitched. 'Lappin,' she exclaimed suddenly; and gave a little cry as if she had found the very word she looked for.

'Lappin, Lappin, King Lappin,' she repeated. It seemed to suit him exactly; he was not Ernest, he was King Lappin. Why? She did not know.

When there was nothing new to talk about on their long solitary walks – and it rained, as everyone had warned them that it would rain; or when they were sitting over the fire in the evening, for it was cold, and the maiden ladies had gone and the fishing man, and the waiter only came if you rang the bell for him, she let her fancy play with the story of the Lappin tribe. Under her hands – she was sewing, he was reading – they became very real, very vivid, very amusing. Ernest put down the paper and helped her. There were the black rabbits and the red;

there were the enemy rabbits and the friendly. There were the wood in which they lived and the outlying prairies and the swamp. Above all there was King Lappin, who, far from having only the one trick – that he twitched his nose – became, as the days passed, an animal of the greatest character. Rosalind was always finding new qualities in him. But above all he was a great hunter.

'And what,' said Rosalind, on the last day of the honeymoon, 'did the King do to-day?'

In fact they had been climbing all day; and she had worn a blister on her heel; but she did not mean that.

'To-day,' said Ernest twitching his nose as he bit the end off his cigar, 'he chased a hare.' He paused; struck a match, and twitched again.

'A woman hare,' he added.

'A white hare!' Rosalind exclaimed, as if she had been expecting this. 'Rather a small hare; silver grey; with big bright eyes?'

'Yes,' said Ernest, looking at her as she had looked at him, 'a smallish animal; with eyes popping out of her head, and two little front paws dangling.' It was exactly how she sat, with her sewing dangling in her hands; and her eyes, that were so big and bright, were certainly a little prominent.

'Ah, Lapinova,' Rosalind murmured.

'Is that what she's called,' said Ernest, 'the real Rosalind?' He looked at her. He felt very much in love with her.

'Yes; that's what she's called,' said Rosalind: 'Lapinova.' And before they went to bed that night it was all settled. He was King Lappin; she was Queen Lapinova. They were the very opposite of each other; he was bold and determined; she wary and undependable. He ruled over the busy world of rabbits; her world was a desolate, mysterious place, which she ranged mostly by moonlight. All the same, their territories touched; they were King and Queen of the land of rabbits and hares.

Thus when they came back from their honeymoon they possessed a private world, inhabited, save for the one white hare, entirely by rabbits. No one guessed that there was such a place, and that of course made it all the more amusing. It made them feel, more even than most young married couples, in league together against the rest of the world. Often they looked slyly at each other when people talked about rabbits and woods and traps and shooting. Or they winked furtively across the table when Aunt Mary said that she could never bear to see a hare in a dish – it looked so like a baby; or when John, Ernest's sporting brother, told them what price rabbits were fetching that autumn in Wiltshire, skins and all. Sometimes when they wanted a gamekeeper, or a poacher or a Lord of the Manor, they amused themselves by distributing the parts among their friends. Ernest's mother, Mrs. Reginald Thorburn, for example, fitted the part of the Squire to perfection. But it was all secret – that was the point of it; nobody save themselves knew that such a world existed.

Without that world, how, Rosalind wondered, could she ever have endured the golden-wedding party[5] when all the Thorburns assembled at Porchester Terrace to celebrate the fiftieth anniversary of that union which had been so blessed – had it not produced Ernest Thorburn? – and so fruitful – had it not produced nine other sons and daughters into the bargain, many themselves married and also fruitful? She dreaded that party. But it was inevitable. As she walked upstairs she felt bitterly that she was an only child and an orphan at that; a mere drop among all those Thorburns assembled in the great drawing-room with the shiny satin wallpaper and the lustrous family portraits. The living Thorburns much resembled the painted; save that instead of painted lips they had real lips; out of which came jokes; jokes about schoolrooms, and how they had pulled the chair from under the governess; jokes about frogs and how they had put them between the virgin sheets of maiden ladies. As for herself, she had never even made an apple-pie bed. Holding her present in her hand, she advanced towards her mother-in-law, sumptuous in yellow satin; and towards her father-in-law, decorated with a rich yellow carnation. All round them on tables and chairs there were golden tributes, some nestling in cotton wool; others branching resplendent – candlesticks; cigar boxes; chains; each stamped with the goldsmith's proof that it was solid gold, hall-marked, authentic. But her present was only a little pinchbeck[6] box pierced with holes; an old sand caster, an eighteenth-century relic, once used to sprinkle sand over wet ink. Rather a senseless present, she felt, in an age of blotting-paper; and as she proffered it, she saw in front of her the stubby black handwriting in which her mother-in-law, when they were engaged, had expressed the hope that 'My son will make you happy.' No, she was not happy. Not at all happy. She looked at Ernest, straight as a ramrod with a nose like all the noses in the family portraits, a nose that never twitched at all.

Then they went down to dinner. She was half hidden by the great chrysanthemums that curled their red and gold petals into large tight balls. Everything was gold. A gold-edged card with gold initials intertwined recited the list of all the dishes that would be set one after another before them. She dipped her spoon in a plate of clear golden soup. The raw white fog outside had been turned by the lamps into a golden mesh that blurred the edges of the plates and gave the pineapples a rough golden skin. Only she herself in her white wedding dress peering ahead of her with her prominent eyes seemed insoluble as an icicle.

As the dinner wore on, however, the room grew steamy with heat. Beads of perspiration stood out on the men's foreheads. She felt that her icicle was being turned to water. She was being melted; dispersed; dissolved into nothingness; and would soon faint. Then through the surge in her head and the din in her ears she heard a woman's voice exclaim, 'But of course they breed so!'

The Thorburns – yes; they breed so, she echoed; looking at all the round red faces that seemed doubled in the giddiness that overcame her; and magnified in the gold mist that enhaloed them. 'They breed so.' Then John bawled:

'Little devils! Shoot 'em! Jump on 'em with big boots! That's the only way to deal with 'em . . . rabbits!'

At that word, that magic word, she revived. Peeping between

the chrysanthemums she saw Ernest's nose twitch. It rippled, it ran, with successive twitches. And at that a mysterious catastrophe befell the Thorburns. The golden table became a moor with the gorse in full bloom; the din of voices turned to one peal of lark's laughter ringing down from the sky. It was a blue sky – clouds passed slowly. And they had all been changed – the Thorburns. She looked at her father-in-law, a furtive little man with dyed moustaches. His foible was collecting things – seals, enamel boxes, trifles from eighteenth-century dressing-tables which he hid from his wife in the drawers of his desk. Now she saw him as he was – a poacher, stealing off with his coat bulging with pheasants and partridges to drop them stealthily into a three-legged pot in his smoky little cottage. That was her real father-in-law – a poacher. And Celia, the unmarried daughter, who always nosed out other people's secrets, the little things they wished to hide – she was a white ferret with pink eyes, and a nose clotted with earth from her horrid underground nosings and pokings. Slung round men's shoulders, in a net, and thrust down a hole – it was a pitiable life, Celia's; it was none of her fault. So she saw Celia. And then she looked at her mother-in-law – whom they dubbed The Squire. Flushed, coarse, a bully – she was all that, as she stood returning thanks, but now that Rosalind – that is Lapinova – saw her, she saw behind her the decayed family mansion, the plaster peeling off the walls, and heard her, with a sob in her voice, giving thanks to her children (who hated her) for a world that had ceased to exist. There was a sudden silence. They all stood with their glasses raised; they all drank; then it was over.

'Oh, King Lappin!' she cried as they went home together in the fog. 'If your nose hadn't twitched just at that moment, I should have been trapped!'

'But you're safe,' said King Lappin, pressing her paw.

'Quite safe,' she answered, pressing his too.

And they drove back through the Park, King and Queen of the marsh, of the mist, of the gorse-scented moor.

*

Thus time passed; one year; two years of time. And on a winter's night, which happened by a coincidence to be the anniversary of the golden-wedding party – but Mrs. Reginald Thorburn was dead; the house was to let; and there was only a caretaker in residence – Ernest came home from the office. They had a nice little home; half a house above a saddler's shop in South Kensington, not far from the tube station.[7] It was cold, with fog in the air, and Rosalind was sitting over the fire, sewing.

'What d'you think happened to me to-day?' she began as soon as he had settled himself down with his legs stretched to the blaze. 'I was crossing the stream when —'

'What stream?' Ernest interrupted her.

'The stream at the bottom, where our wood meets the black wood,' she explained.

Ernest looked completely blank for a moment.

'What the deuce are you talking about?' he asked.

'My dear Ernest!' she cried in dismay. 'King Lappin,' she added, dangling her little front paws in the firelight. But his nose did not twitch. Her hands – they turned to hands – clutched the stuff she was holding; her eyes popped half out of her head. It took him five minutes at least to change from Ernest Thorburn to King Lappin; and while she waited she felt a load on the back of her neck, as if somebody were about to wring it. At last he changed to King Lappin; his nose twitched; and they spent the evening roaming the woods much as usual.

But she slept badly. In the middle of the night she woke, feeling as if something strange had happened to her. She was stiff and cold. At last she turned on the light and looked at Ernest lying beside her. He was sound asleep. He snored. But even though he snored, his nose remained perfectly still. It looked as if it had never twitched at all. Was it possible that he was really Ernest; and that she was really married to Ernest? A vision of her mother-in-law's dining-room came before her; and there they sat, she and Ernest, grown old, under the engravings, in front of the sideboard. . . . It was their golden-wedding day. She could not bear it.

'Lappin, King Lappin!' she whispered, and for a moment his nose seemed to twitch of its own accord. But he still slept. 'Wake up, Lappin, wake up!' she cried.

Ernest woke; and, seeing her sitting bolt upright beside him, he asked:

'What's the matter?'

'I thought my rabbit was dead!' she whimpered. Ernest was angry.

'Don't talk such rubbish, Rosalind,' he said. 'Lie down and go to sleep.'

He turned over. In another moment he was sound asleep and snoring.

But she could not sleep. She lay curled up on her side of the bed, like a hare in its form. She had turned out the light, but the street-lamp lit the ceiling faintly, and the trees outside made a lacy network over it as if there were a shadowy grove on the ceiling in which she wandered, turning, twisting, in and out, round and round, hunting, being hunted, hearing the bay of hounds, and horns blowing . . . until the maid drew the blinds and brought their early tea.

Next day she could settle to nothing. She seemed to have lost something. She felt as if her body had shrunk; it had grown small, and black and hard. Her joints seemed stiff too, and when she looked in the glass, which she did several times as she wandered about the flat, her eyes seemed to burst out of her head, like currants in a bun. The rooms also seemed to have shrunk. Large pieces of furniture jutted out at odd angles and she found herself knocking against them. At last she put on her hat and went out. She walked along the Cromwell Road; and every room she passed and peered into seemed to be a dining-room where people sat eating under steel engravings, with thick yellow lace curtains, and mahogany sideboards. At last she reached the Natural History Museum;[8] she used to like it when she was a child. But the first thing she saw when she went in was a stuffed hare standing on sham snow with pink glass eyes. Somehow it made her shiver all over. Perhaps it would be better when dusk fell. She went home and sat over the fire, without a light, and tried to imagine that she was out alone on a moor: and there was a stream rushing; and beyond the stream a dark wood. But she could get no farther than the stream. At last she squatted down on the bank on the wet grass, and sat crouched in her chair, with her hands dangling empty, and her eyes glazed, like glass eyes, in the firelight. Then there was the crack of a gun . . . She started as if she had been shot. It was only Ernest turning his key in the door. She waited, trembling. He came in and switched on the light. There he stood tall, handsome, rubbing his hands that were red with cold.

'Sitting in the dark?' he said.

'Oh, Ernest, Ernest!' she cried starting up in her chair.

'Well, what's up now?' he asked briskly, warming his hands at the fire.

'It's Lapinova . . .' she faltered, glancing wildly at him out of her great startled eyes. 'She's gone, Ernest. I've lost her!'

Ernest frowned. He pressed his lips tight together. 'Oh, that's what's up, is it?' he said, smiling rather grimly at his wife. For ten seconds he stood there, silent; and she waited, feeling hands tightening at the back of her neck.

'Yes,' he said at length. 'Poor Lapinova . . .' He straightened his tie at the looking-glass.

'Caught in a trap,' he said. 'Killed,' and sat down and read the newspaper.

So that was the end of that marriage.

Notes

A HAUNTED HOUSE

First published in *Monday or Tuesday* (1921), from which this text has been reprinted, and posthumously in *A Haunted House and Other Short Stories* (1944).

The story was inspired by Asham (or Asheham) House, near Firle, on the South Downs, which Virginia and Leonard Woolf had discovered together and bought. They spent weekends and holidays there from 1912–19. The house was supposed to be haunted:

> It sounded as if two people were walking from room to room, opening and shutting doors, sighing, whispering . . . I have never known a house which had such a strong character, personality of its own – romantic, gentle, melancholy, lovely. It was Asham and its ghostly footsteps and whisperings which gave Virginia the idea for 'A Haunted House', and I can immediately see, hear, and smell the house when I read the opening words.
> Leonard Woolf, *An Autobiography* (II, 1911–19, OUP, 1980, p. 37).

Two or three days after the publication of *Monday or Tuesday*, Woolf wrote 'one begins to wish one had put in other stories – or left out the Haunted House, which may be sentimental.' Yet it was much admired by reviewers, and T. S. Eliot singled it out as 'extremely interesting' (see *Diary*, II, 10 April, 3 May, 7 June 1921, pp. 108, 116, 125).

A SOCIETY

Published in *Monday or Tuesday* and not reprinted.

In September 1920 Arnold Bennett published *Our Women: Chapters on the Sex-Discord*. Its argument, that women were intellectually inferior to men, provoked Woolf to make up 'a paper upon Women, as a counterblast to Mr Bennett's adverse views reported in the papers' (*Diary*, II, 26 Sept. 1920, p. 69). 'A Society' may be that paper. Woolf also corresponded with Desmond MacCarthy in the *New Statesman* over Bennett's book; their respective contributions are reprinted in *A Woman's Essays* (Penguin Books, 1992, pp. 30–39). The question of women's intellectual inferiority and the importance of Sappho as a major woman poet are raised there. Other themes – the critique of male institutions, men's responsibility for war, their insistence on women's chastity ('casta' is the Latin for 'chaste', thus Castalia is unfortunately named), and their pleasure in 'stars of all shapes, ribbons of all shades' – were not fully explored until *Three Guineas* (1938; reprinted with *A Room of One's Own*, Penguin Books, 1993).

1. *all the books in the London Library*: Woolf's father, Leslie Stephen, was a great supporter of the Library, and latterly became its president.
2. *'From a Window' . . . Benton or Henson*: the title and author's name suggest A. C. Benson's *From a College Window* (1906).
3. *Ethiopian Prince . . . ships*: in February 1910, Virginia Stephen, with her brother Adrian, Duncan Grant, Horace Cole and Guy Ridley, took part in the 'Dreadnought Hoax', in which Cole posed as the Emperor of Abyssinia, who, with his train, paid an official visit of inspection to HMS *Dreadnought*. Virginia's first cousin, William Fisher, was Flag Commander of the ship, and he subsequently punished Duncan Grant with two ceremonious taps on the bottom (see Quentin Bell, *Virginia Woolf*, I, pp. 157–61, 213–16).
4. *'O for the touch . . . glory –'*: the sources of Helen's (not always accurate) quotations are as follows: 'But O for the touch of a vanish'd hand/And the sound of a voice that is still!', from Alfred Lord Tennyson's 'Break, Break, Break'; 'Home is the sailor, home from the sea,/And the hunter home from the hill', from Robert Louis Stevenson's *Underwoods* (xxi, Requiem); 'He gave his bridle reins a shake', from Robert Burns's 'It was a' for our Rightfu' King'; 'Love is sweet, love is brief' has not been identified; 'Spring, the sweet spring, is the year's pleasant king' is the opening of a song by Thomas Nashe from his play *Summer's Last Will and Testament*; 'Oh, to be in England/Now that April's there' is the opening of Robert Browning's 'Home-Thoughts, from Abroad'; 'For men must work, and women must weep', from Charles Kingsley's 'The

Three Fishers'; 'The path of duty was the way to glory', from Alfred Lord Tennyson's 'Ode on the Death of the Duke of Wellington' (viii).

5. *Once . . . the Aloe flowered*: in Katherine Mansfield's story 'Prelude', Kezia's mother tells her that the aloe flowers once every hundred years. 'Prelude' was the second book to be published by Virginia and Leonard Woolf at the Hogarth Press, in 1918.
6. *an edition of Sappho*: born on Lesbos in 612 BC, Sappho was one of the earliest and most famous of lyric poets. A number of her love poems were addressed to women.
7. *an invention of hers . . . to bear children —*: Judith, in anticipating the possiblity of condom machines and artificial insemination, foresees ways in which the women of the future will be able to exercise greater control over their own fertility.
8. *I have read new books . . . Mr. Walpole*: Elizabeth's experiences as a reviewer parallel those of Woolf herself. H. G. Wells (1866–1946) was perhaps the best-known novelist and polemicist of his day. Woolf reviewed his novel *Joan and Peter* for *The Times Literary Supplement* (1918; see *Essays*, II, pp. 294–7). Arnold Bennett (1867–1931) was a novelist whose social realism Woolf repeatedly criticized, and whose book *Our Women* (1920) probably occasioned this story. Compton Mackenzie (1883–1972) is best-known for *Sinister Street* (1913–14); its sequels, *Sylvia Scarlett* (1918) and *Sylvia and Michael* (1919), were both reviewed by Woolf (see *Essays*, II, pp. 288–91; *Essays*, III, pp. 20–21). Stephen McKenna (1888–1956) made his reputation with his novel *Sonia* (1917); Woolf reviewed the sequel *Sonia Married* (1919), (see *Essays*, III, pp. 95–6), as she did *The Green Mirror* (1918) by Hugh Walpole (1884–1941), who was another popular novelist of the day (see *Essays*, II, pp. 214–17).
9. *War! Declaration of War!*: on 4 August 1914 Britain declared war on Germany. The events of that afternoon are recorded in Chapter 13 of *Jacob's Room*, (1922; Penguin Books, 1992, esp. pp. 150–53).
10. *Mr. Lloyd George*: Liberal Prime Minister from 1916–22.
11. *The Treaty of Peace . . . signed*: the Treaty of Versailles between Germany and the allies was signed on 28 June 1919, thus formally bringing the First World War to an end. References to the Treaty in the opening paragraphs of 'An Unwritten Novel' and 'The String Quartet' suggest that Woolf intended it to provide a unifying historical moment for *Monday or Tuesday*.

MONDAY OR TUESDAY

First published in *Monday or Tuesday*, in this version, and reprinted posthumously in *A Haunted House*.

Woolf seems to have planned this as the title of the whole book before she actually wrote the story: in a letter to her sister Vanessa on 31 October 1920, she adds in a postscript, 'I'm getting doubtful whether I have time to write the story called Monday or Tuesday – if not, I don't know what to call the book' (*Letters*, II, p. 445). When Woolf came to rewrite her essay 'Modern Novels' (1919, *Essays*, III, pp. 30–37) for inclusion in *The Common Reader* (1925), as 'Modern Fiction', she introduced the phrase 'the life of Monday or Tuesday' into the passage describing 'The mind, exposed to the ordinary course of life' as an allusion to her book.

Like 'Blue and Green', 'Monday or Tuesday', is a kind of prose poem. Woolf was later to write dismissively of both pieces to Ethel Smyth (*Letters*, IV, 16 Oct. 1930, p. 231):

> You are perfectly right about Green and blue and the heron one [i.e. 'Monday or Tuesday']: thats mainly why I won't reprint. They are mere tangles of words; balls of string that the kitten or Pan [Ethel's dog] has played with . . . Green and Blue and the heron were the wild outbursts of freedom, inarticulate, ridiculous, unprintable mere outcries.

1. *a cry starts . . . it is mid-day*: this sequence of sentences had earlier been used by Woolf in an unpublished short story, 'Sympathy', which Susan Dick suggests was written at the end of April 1919 (it is reprinted in *Virginia Woolf: The Complete Shorter Fiction*, ed. Dick, Hogarth Press, 1985; rev. 1989, p. 110).
2. *Flaunted, leaf-light . . . assembled*: this passage suggests the influence of Gerard Manley Hopkins, whose poems were first published in 1918. On 23 July 1919, Woolf wrote to Janet Case:

   > Have you read the poems of a man, who is dead, called Gerard Hopkins? I liked them better than any poetry for ever so long; partly because they're so difficult, but also because instead of writing mere rhythms and sense as most poets do, he makes a very strange jumble; so that what is apparently pure nonsense

> is at the same time very beautiful, and not nonsense at all. Now this carries out a theory of mine . . .

On 5 January 1920, she sent Janet Case the poems, quoting 'Heaven-Haven' and adding 'Yes, I should like to have written that myself' (*Letters*, II, pp. 379, 415).

AN UNWRITTEN NOVEL

First published in the *London Mercury* in July 1920; it was slightly revised for *Monday or Tuesday* (the version adopted here) and posthumously reprinted in *A Haunted House*.

'An Unwritten Novel' must have been written by 26 January 1920, since Woolf, trying to visualize her next novel (*Jacob's Room*), wrote in her diary (II, pp. 13–14):

> Suppose one thing should open out of another – as in An Unwritten Novel – only not for 10 pages but 200 or so – doesn't that give the looseness and lightness I want . . . but conceive mark on the wall, K[ew]. G[ardens]. & unwritten novel taking hands and dancing in unity. What the unity shall be I have yet to discover: the theme is a blank to me; but I see immense possibilities in the form . . .

Like the unpublished short story 'Sympathy', 'An Unwritten Novel' describes the process of fictional reconstruction. Woolf often associated this with imagining the characters of passengers on train journeys, as for example in Chapter III of *Jacob's Room* (1921; Penguin Books, 1992, pp. 23–4), or in her essay 'Mr Bennett and Mrs Brown' (*A Woman's Essays*, Penguin Books, 1992, pp. 72–5; see also the unfinished 'Byron and Mr. Briggs', *Essays*, III, pp. 474–99).

1. *the map of the line framed opposite*: a framed map of the railway line was displayed above the seats. The journey from London to Eastbourne, passes through Three Bridges and Lewes. Woolf was familiar with this journey, which took her down to Asheham House (see the note on 'A Haunted House', above).
2. *Peace between . . . Minister*: see 'A Society', Note 11, above. On 19

June 1919, Signor Nitti accepted an invitation from the Italian king to become Premier and form a coalition ministry, which survived until 1 December.

3. *some spot between her shoulders burnt or itched*: a diary entry for 4 February 1920 records that Leonard and the Woolfs' maid, Lottie Hope, were both suffering from itches. Woolf comments, 'But imagination! By taking thought I can itch at any point on my hundreds of inches of skin. I do it now' (*Diary*, II, p. 17). Minnie Marsh's itch, however, seems to resemble Lady Macbeth's imaginary spot of blood in that it is associated with guilt, created on an occasion when she was attracted by violet ribbons in a shop window and returned late to find that some domestic disaster had taken place.
4. *President Kruger than Prince Albert*: Kruger, who led the Boers against the English in 1880, was dark with bristling black whiskers, 'a brutal old bully'. He would have made a harsh and Calvinist deity in comparison to the slender and graceful Prince Albert, consort to Queen Victoria.
5. *from the basement; dot, dot, dot*: Woolf was always amused by the literary convention of three dots: a diary entry plans to end *Orlando* 'with three dots . . . so' (14 March 1927, *Diary*, III, p. 131), and there are similar self-conscious uses in *Three Guineas*. Rachel Bowlby in *Virginia Woolf: Feminist Destinations* (Blackwell, 1988) discusses Woolf's various uses of the convention (pp. 160–70), as well as her use of the device of the train journey (pp. 1–16).
6. *glacis*: a sloping bank or parapet.

Note: In revising 'An Unwritten Novel' for publication in *Monday or Tuesday*, Woolf made the following cuts:

p. 29, line 15: Shallow trays brim with ribbons [all along the counters]. She pauses.

p. 30, line 8: . . . it seems as if washing helped. [You take the sponge, the pumice-stone, you scrape and scrub, you squirm and sluice; it can't be done – let *me* try; I can't reach it either – the spot between the shoulders – cold water only – why should she grudge that?] And John at breakfast –

p. 32, line 33: eating her egg at the moment opposite [(I can't bear to watch her!)] and at t'other end of the line –

THE STRING QUARTET

Published in *Monday or Tuesday* in the version reproduced here, and posthumously in *A Haunted House*.

On 7 March 1920, Woolf went to Campden Hill 'to hear the S[c]hubert quintet – to see George Booth's house – to take notes for my story – to rub shoulders with respectability – all these reasons took me there, & were cheaply gratified at 7/6' (*Diary*, II, p. 24). The resultant story may owe something to E. M. Forster's imaginative treatment of a concert in Chapter V of *Howard's End* (1910). Her diary for 7 June 1921 records that T. S. Eliot 'picked out the String Quartet, especially the end of it. "Very good" he said, and meant it, I think' (*Diary*, II, p. 125).

1. *landaus with bays*: carriages with folding roofs, drawn by bay (i.e., chestnut) horses – an expensive and exclusive mode of transport.
2. *that Regent Street . . . influenza*: on the Treaty, see 'A Society', Note 11, above. Regent Street, a wide street of large department stores in the West End, was 'up', i.e. closed for repairs. There was a serious epidemic of Spanish influenza in 1919.
3. *old jolly fishwives . . . women*: the delirious Rachel thinks she sees 'Little deformed women sitting in archways playing cards' in Chapter XXV of *The Voyage Out* (1915; Penguin Books, 1992, p. 313).
4. *Sorrow . . . Woven together*: perhaps echoing Blake's 'Auguries of Innocence': 'Joy and woe are woven fine,/A clothing for the soul divine.'

BLUE AND GREEN

Published in *Monday or Tuesday*, in this version, and not reprinted (see introductory note to 'Monday or Tuesday', above).

Like 'Monday or Tuesday', 'Blue and Green' is a fantasy whose starting point seems to be a lustre, a Victorian ornament made up of suspended glass prisms, that stands on the marble mantelpiece. As the light changes from day to night, so the lustre changes from throwing off green to blue reflections.

S. P. Rosenbaum has pointed out that these two sketches seem to be exercises in the rendering of consciousness, relating them to the philosopher G. E. Moore's essay 'The Refutation of Idealism' (1903), in which Moore describes consciousness as follows:

> The term 'blue' is easy enough to distinguish, but the other element which I have called 'consciousness' – that which sensation of blue has in common with sensation of green – is extremely difficult to fix. That many people fail to distinguish it at all is sufficiently shown by the fact that there are materialists. And, in general, that which makes the sensation of blue a mental fact seems to escape us: it seems, if I may use a metaphor, to be transparent – we look through it and see nothing but the blue; we may be convinced that there *is something* but *what* it is no philosopher, I think, has yet clearly recognized.
>
> (See S. P. Rosenbaum, 'The Philosophical Realism of Virginia Woolf', in S. P. Rosenbaum, (ed.) *English Literature and British Philosophy*, Chicago University Press, 1971, pp. 320–3).

KEW GARDENS

This story was first published by the Hogarth Press on 12 May 1919, in an edition of 150. After an enthusiastic review in *The Times Literary Supplement*, it rapidly sold out, and was reprinted in the following month in an edition of 500. Both editions were illustrated with woodcuts by Vanessa Bell. It was then included in *Monday or Tuesday*, in the version reprinted here. A third, limited edition of *Kew Gardens* was published by the Hogarth Press in 1927, and it appeared in *A Haunted House*.

Woolf must have been working on a version of this story as early as August 1917, when Katherine Mansfield wrote to her, 'Yes, your Flower Bed is very good. There's a still quivering changing light over it all and a sense of these couples dissolving in the bright air which fascinates me'. *The Collected Letters of Katherine Mansfield*, ed. Vincent O'Sullivan and Margaret Scott (OUP, 1984, Vol. I, 1903–1917, p. 327).

Woolf wrote to Vanessa about it on 25 June 1918, saying 'It seems to me very bad now, and not worth printing, but I'll send it to you if you like – I thought perhaps I could rewrite it', and a few days later, 'I'm sending my story; you will see that it's a case of atmosphere, and I don't think I've got it quite. Don't you think you might design a title page? Tell me what you think of the story' (1 July 1918, *Letters*, II, pp. 225, 257).

The Woolfs had moved to Richmond in 1914, and the Royal Botanic Gardens at Kew soon became a favourite walk, as Virginia's diary indicates: on 26 November 1917 she writes of the tropical orchids, 'They always make me anxious to bring them into a novel' (*Diary*, I, p. 82). The gardens and the orchid house were to figure in Chapter XXV of *Night and Day* (1919; Penguin Books, 1992, pp. 279–82) as the setting in which Ralph and Katharine first recognize their physical attraction; in Chapter 6 of *Orlando* (1929; Penguin Books, 1993, p. 203) Kew is associated with fecundity ('to walk there is to be thinking of bulbs, hairy and red, thrust into the earth in October; flowering now; and to be dreaming of more than can rightly be said').

1. *forests of Uruguay . . . women drowned at sea*: the dreamy combination of South America, a beautiful young woman and images of women drowning suggest aspects of Woolf's first novel, *The Voyage Out* (1915; Penguin Books, 1992).
2. '*They make you pay sixpence on Friday*': i.e. for entry to the Botanic Gardens. The entry charge was 1d, except for Thursdays and Fridays, when it was 6d. On Friday 23 November 1917, Woolf 'settled that if it was the 6d day at Kew I wouldn't hesitate but decide not to go in. It was the 6d day; I turned without pausing and had therefore to walk back. Certainly this decision brings a feeling of peace, though I rather think I was wrong' (*Diary*, I, p. 81).

THE MARK ON THE WALL

With Leonard Woolf's 'Three Jews', this was published as *Two Stories* in July 1917, the first volume printed at the Hogarth Press, in an issue of 150 copies, with woodcuts by Dora Carrington. It was subsequently reprinted separately in June 1919, and in a slightly revised version in *Monday or Tuesday*, in the text adopted here. It was later included in *A Haunted House*.

In a letter to Ethel Smyth, Woolf wrote 'I shall never forget the day I wrote The Mark on the Wall – all in a flash, as if flying' (16 Oct.

[1930], *Letters*, IV, p. 231). E. M. Forster quoted a paragraph from it in the introductory chapter of his *Aspects of the Novel* (1927), defining Woolf, along with Laurence Sterne, as a fantasist. Many of the themes and tones found here recur in her later work, particularly in *Orlando* (1929; Penguin Books, 1993).

1. *asphodel meadows*: the fields of Elysium, where the dead go, according to classical mythology (asphodel is a lily-like flower, associated with immortality).
2. *as one can believe*: at this point *Two Stories* and the version of 1919 included a further paragraph omitted from the text of *Monday or Tuesday*:

> as one can believe. [But I know a housekeeper, a woman with the profile of a police-man, those little round buttons marked even upon the edge of her shadow, a woman with a broom in her hand, a thumb on picture frames, an eye under beds and she talks always of art. She is coming nearer and nearer; and now, pointing to certain spots of yellow rust on the fender, she becomes so menacing that to oust her, I shall have to get up and see for myself what that mark –
>
> But no. I refuse to be beaten. I will not move. I will not recognize her. See, she fades already. I am very nearly rid of her and her insinuations, which I can hear quite distinctly. Yet she has about her the pathos of all people who wish to compromise. And why should I resent the fact that she has a few books in her house, a picture or two? But what I really resent is that she resents me – life being an affair of attack and defence after all. Another time I will have it out with her, not now. She must go now.] The tree outside the window taps very gently on the pane.

3. *Whitaker's Table of Precedency*: Whitaker's *Almanack* provides tables of precedency (though not under that title) for the Royal Family, the Royal Household, the Peerage, the Privy Council, Government and Public Offices, Religious Bodies, etc. Woolf wrote with irritation of the very few women who appeared on these lists in *Three Guineas* (1938).
4. *and the Landseer prints*: Sir Edwin Landseer (1802–73), the Royal Academician, was famous for his paintings of animals and wildlife,

such as 'The Monarch of the Glen'. Reproduced as prints, these often decorated Victorian middle-class homes.

5. *South Downs . . . either tombs or camps*: Woolf seems to be thinking of the landscape around Asham (see introduction to 'A Haunted House', above). In Chapter IV of *Night and Day*, which Woolf was working on from 1916 to 1918, looking at her sofas which resemble 'grassy mounds in their lack of shape . . . Mary [Datchet] was led to think of the heights of a Sussex down, and the swelling green circle of some camp of ancient warriors' (1919; Penguin Books, 1992, p. 37).

SOLID OBJECTS

This appeared in the *Athenaeum* on 22 October 1920, in the version reproduced here, and was later reprinted in *A Haunted House*.

This story is a variant on Woolf's recurrent dilemma, 'Now is life very solid, or very shifting? I am haunted by the two contradictions' (4 January 1929, *Diary*, III, p. 218). In a letter to Vanessa of 26 November 1918, Woolf summarized the opening sequence in terms of a picture for possible illustration:

> I've just started another story, which may never be finished, or may go wrong; so I don't think its worth your while to do a design, though if it comes off, I hope you might do a picture for it – in fact I mean to retain your services for *all* my works. The story begins with two young men sitting on a beach under the skeleton of an old pilchard boat. One young man is throwing stones into the sea; the other is burrowing a hole in the sand. The beach is a long semi circular one, and they are quite near the sea (as of course they must be to throw stones into it).
>
> (*Letters*, II, p. 299)

The hero's obsession with solid objects may owe something to Woolf's impression of the artist Mark Gertler (1891–1939): 'Form obsesses him. He sees a lamp as an imminent dominant overwhelming mass of matter. Ever since he was a child the solidity & the shapes of objects have tortured him' (29 July 1918, *Diary*, I, p. 176). After its publication, Woolf told Hope Mirrlees, 'I'm glad you liked my story. It was written too quick, but I thought it had some points as a way of telling a story' ([late October 1920], *Letters*, VI, p. 497).

IN THE ORCHARD

First published in April 1923, in the *Criterion*, a periodical edited by T. S. Eliot, in this version; subsequently in *Broom*, New York, September 1923, and eventually in *Books and Portraits* (1977).

This is an experimental piece in which Miranda's afternoon in the orchard is described from three different viewpoints. Woolf apparently wrote it during the summer of 1922, when a diary entry for 23 June declares 'I am going to be well on with a story for Eliot' (*Diary*, II, p. 178); a letter to her friend Ka Arnold-Forster on 23 August recommends that she should take the *Criterion* – 'Besides it will have a story, I think, by me' (*Letters*, II, p. 549).

1. *Ce pays . . . le mieux*: the source of this quotation has not been located. It means: 'This country is actually one of the corners of the world where young girls burst into laughter most readily'.
2. *Hymns Ancient and Modern*: the standard hymn book used in Church of England services.
3. *fieldfares*: a species of thrush that migrates to England for the winter (the story is set on a warm day in autumn, when apples and blackberries are ready to be picked and the fieldfares have just returned).
4. *being churched*: i.e. they were attending a service designed to purify or cleanse them after the process of giving birth.
5. *the golden feather of the church tower*: i.e. the weather-vane.

A WOMAN'S COLLEGE FROM OUTSIDE

First published in November 1926 in *Atalanta's Garland: Being the Book of the Edinburgh University Women's Union* in the version reprinted here, and subsequently in *Books and Portraits* (1977).

This story was originally intended to form a chapter of *Jacob's Room*, an account of Newnham to counterbalance that of Trinity, as it were. It may be linked to 'In the Orchard', since draft versions suggest that the heroine was originally to have been called Miranda.

1. *the feathering – white moon . . . the meadows*: this sentence also appears in *Jacob's Room* (1922; Penguin Books, 1992, p.30), where it would presumably have introduced this episode, had it been retained.

2. *this lily floating flawless*: Woolf may be thinking of the Biblical injunction, 'Consider the lilies of the field, how they grow; they toil not, neither do they spin: And yet I say unto you, That even Solomon in all his glory was not arrayed like one of these' (Matt., 6:28). Though lily-like, 'Angela Williams was at Newnham for the purpose of earning her living'.
3. *her father at Swansea*: Swansea is a town on the west coast of Wales (Williams can often be a Welsh name).
4. *Bamborough Castle*: stands on a beautiful but bleak stretch of coast to the far north-east of England, close to the Scottish border.

THE LADY IN THE LOOKING-GLASS: A REFLECTION

This story was first published in *Harper's Magazine* in December 1929, in the version reproduced here. In the following year it appeared in *Harper's Bazaar* (New York, January 1930), and posthumously in *A Haunted House*.

One starting point for this story was provided by Woolf's friend Ethel Sands, (1873–1962), a famous hostess, patron and painter, born in America, but now dividing her time between Chelsea and the Château d'Auppegard in Normandy, where Woolf visited her at the end of July 1927: 'It is a very narrow house, all windows, laid with pale bright Samarcand rugs, & painted greens & blues, with lovely 'pieces', & great pots of carefully designed flowers arranged by Loomas [the butler]' (8 August 1927, *Diary*, III, p. 151). On 20 September, Woolf wrote, 'How many little stories come into my head! For instance: Ethel Sands not looking at her letters. What this implies. One might write a book of short significant separate scenes. She did not open her letters' (*Diary*, III, p. 157). This sentence became the last line of the story in her original draft: 'Isabella did not open her letters'. The earliest surviving draft, however, is dated 28 May 1929, when she was struggling to begin the novel that was to become *The Waves*: 'How am I to begin it? And what is it to be? I feel no great impulse; no fever; only a great pressure of difficulty. Why write it then? Why write at all? Every morning I write a little sketch, to amuse myself' (28 May 1929, *Diary*, III, p. 229).

Like 'An Unwritten Novel', 'The Lady in the Looking-Glass' is based on a contrast between the richness and fullness of the creative imagination and the flatness or emptiness of daily experience. The subtitle, 'A Reflection', points to the way the mirror and the reflecting mind can defamiliarize or make mysterious the life of the room (which also resembles the life of the mind), but in the story's final moments, the magic of the transforming gaze is abruptly withdrawn.

THE SHOOTING PARTY

This story was published in *Harper's Bazaar* (London and New York) for March 1938 in the version used here, and posthumously in *A Haunted House*.

The idea for 'The Shooting Party' came to Woolf in the months following the publication of *The Waves*: on 29 December 1931 she wrote:

> Shall I ever 'write' again? And what is writing? The perpetual converse I keep up. I've stopped it these 5 or 6 weeks . . . Books come gently surging round me, like icebergs. I could write a book of caricatures. Christabel's story of the Hall Caines suggested a caricature of Country house life, with the red-brown pheasants . . .
>
> (*Diary*, IV, p. 57)

Christabel McLaren (later Lady Aberconway) was a London hostess, and a fund of gossip; Hall Caine was an immensely successful popular novelist, who had died earlier that year. In January 1932 Woolf drew up a proposed list of 'caricatures': 'The Shooting Party. /2. Scenes from English life/The pheasants/Scenes: Life on a Battleship': a revised list drawn up in February includes 'Country House Life', 'The Royal Navy' and 'The Great Jeweller'. Draft versions of the story are dated 19 January 1932, but do not include the first and the last two paragraphs.

Woolf revised the story for publication in the autumn of 1937, when she was having difficulty finishing *Three Guineas*. It seems likely that she added the framing train journey at this stage, a device she had earlier used in 'An Unwritten Novel', which also features a mysterious woman in a train. The woman's initials, M. M., which identify her as 'Milly Masters, the housekeeper' of the main story, are also those of the (imaginary) 'Minnie Marsh' of 'An Unwritten Novel'. A diary entry for

19 October 1937 reveals Woolf thinking about further possible ways of developing the story:

> It came over me suddenly last night, as I was reading The Shooting Party, – the story that I'm to send to America, H[arper's]. B[azaar]., that I saw the form of a new novel. Its to be first the statement of the theme: then the restatement: & so on: repeating the same story: singling out this & then that: until the central idea is stated . . .
>
> What happened was this: when I finished the S. P. I thought, now that the woman has called a taxi; I will go on to meet, say Christabel [McLaren], at T[avistock]. Square who tells the story again: or I will expatiate upon my own idea in telling the story; or I will find some other person at the S. P. whose life I will tell: but all the scenes must be controlled, & radiate to a centre. I think this is a possible idea; & wd. admit of doing it in short bursts: cd. be a concentrated small book: cd. contain many varieties of mood.
>
> (*Diary*, V, p. 114)

1. *coloured photograph of York Minster*: railway carriages used to be decorated with photographs of beauty spots and famous buildings such as York Cathedral.
2. *'Edward' . . . flourish beneath*: a photograph of King Edward VII, who reigned from 1901–10, and enjoyed country-house shooting parties.
3. *the hanger*: a wood on the side of a steep hill.
4. *old Miss Rashleigh*: the use of her surname indicates that she is Miss Antonia's elder sister. The family line is dying out with these two old maids, and their (younger?) brother the Squire, who has only left illegitimate children (such as Milly Masters's son). As the housekeeper herself comments (ostensibly on the dead pheasants), 'The last of the lot!'

THE DUCHESS AND THE JEWELLER

This story was published in *Harper's Bazaar* (London) for April 1938, in the version given here, and in the following month in the New York edition of *Harper's Bazaar*; it was reprinted in *A Haunted House*.

Woolf's list of possible 'Caricatures' compiled in February 1931 (see introductory note to 'The Shooting Party') included one of 'The Great

Jeweller', although drafts of the text and references to it seem to date from August 1937. On 17 August Virginia wrote to Vanessa:

> You were right about the American magazine: they now say they will take my story if I wire a suitable synopsis – which is a sketch of the plot; so I've made up a story about a jeweller and a duchess, and cabled the plot – how he buys her pearls, for £10,000, knowing them to be false – thats not all of it by any means . . . I am completely stuck on my war pamphlet [i.e. *Three Guineas*], so I may as well write about Duchesses.
>
> (*Letters*, VI, p. 159)

A diary entry for the same day records

> a moment of the old rapture – think of it! – over copying The Duchess & The Jeweller, for Chambrun NY [Jacques Chambrun was a New York literary agent]. I had to send a synopsis. I expect he'll regret the synopsis. But there was the old excitement, even in that little extravagant flash –
>
> (*Diary*, V, p. 107)

A month later, a note of unease emerges in a letter to Vanessa mentioning that Chambrun wants to see her, 'which means I expect he wants to shuffle out of the Jew and the duchess, as well he may' (24 Sept. 1937, *Letters*, VI, p. 173). Chambrun, having approved of the synopsis, was unhappy with the story's evident anti-Semitism. Specific references to 'a little Jew boy' and 'crowds of Jewesses' were subsequently omitted, and the protagonist's name was changed from 'Isadore Oliver' to 'Oliver Bacon', but the reference to his nose ('long and flexible, like an elephant's trunk') and even the revised name 'Bacon' (Jews are forbidden to eat pork) remained. It is difficult to understand why Woolf, who was happily married to a Jew for nearly thirty years, should have written thus, and particularly at this time when Jews were being systematically persecuted in Germany, but the story probably contains elements of oddly displaced anger. She had been intensely distressed at the news of her nephew Julian's death in Spain, a month earlier, and wrote (or perhaps revised) this story before she had recovered from the shock.

1. *Green Park*: a park lying between Piccadilly, and Buckingham Palace in London's West End – a particularly expensive and upper-class area in which to live.

2. *Savile Row*: lying between Regent Street and Bond Street, Savile Row is traditionally associated with the best gentlemen's tailors.
3. *Whitechapel . . . done*: an area in London's poor East End largely inhabited by immigrants – in the first half of this century, these were predominantly East European Jews, who frequently clashed with Fascist gangs during the 1930s. Woolf's *Flush: a Biography* (1933) identifies Whitechapel with the stealing and re-selling of dogs to fashionable women when Elizabeth Barrett's spaniel Flush becomes a victim of this practice. 'Once he had been done' means 'he had been duped, swindled'.
4. *Hatton Garden*: a street to the north-west of Holborn Circus, famous for its diamond merchants.
5. *hansom cab . . . Richmond*: a hansom was a two-wheeled carriage, with the driver's seat behind, and the reins passing over the roof. Richmond is an attractive suburb to the south-west of London, where the Woolfs had lived from 1914 to 1924.
6. *Bond Street*: an expensive shopping street in the heart of Mayfair, the setting for the opening scenes of Woolf's *Mrs Dalloway* (1925; Penguin Books, 1992).
7. *shagreen*: untanned leather with an artificially granulated surface, usually dyed dark green.
8. *the Appleby cincture*: a famous (fictional) family jewel, in the form either of a girdle or a headband.

LAPPIN AND LAPINOVA

This story was published in *Harper's Bazaar* (London and New York) for April 1939, in the version reprinted here, and later in *A Haunted House*.

On 30 October 1938, soon after the publication of *Three Guineas*, Woolf noted in her diary, 'Asked to write a story for Harpers'. Three weeks later, she records, 'I mean to write Reflections on my position as a writer . . . have 10 minutes over from reshaping Lappin & Lapinova, a story written I think at Asheham 20 years ago or more: when I was writing Night & Day perhaps.' Later entries that week record, 'the bore of writing out a story to make money', and 'More brain churning to add a passage to L & L'. But by 18 January 1939 the story had been accepted by *Harper's*: 'I heard this morning. A beautiful story, enchanted to have it' (*Diary*, V, pp. 183, 188, 189, 200).

Like *Night and Day* (1919; Penguin Books, 1992) 'Lappin and Lapinova' is concerned with the relationship between lovers and their imaginary worlds, and like that novel, it was partly inspired by Leonard and Virginia's courtship, in which they played different animals ('Mongoose' and 'Mandrill', as Lyndall Gordon records in *Virginia Woolf: A Writer's Life*, 1984, p. 142). The survival of a marriage, the story implies, might depend upon the maintenance of its inner fantasy world. The story also reveals Rosalind's limited life both as a girl and a woman: like Rachel Vinrace in *The Voyage Out* (1915; Penguin Books, 1992, p. 197), she had been brought up to feed the rabbits, and her married life seems to afford little more than a fantasy life, by way of occupation.

1. *Eton jackets*: short black coats, reaching only to the waist, and named after the uniform of Eton, England's most famous private school for boys.
2. *hotel . . . to the mountains*: the couple are evidently in Switzerland, a favourite place for a honeymoon.
3. *Albert Memorial . . . Porchester Terrace*: the Albert Memorial is an elaborate Gothic structure in Kensington Gardens, erected by Queen Victoria in memory of her husband Albert, the Prince Consort. Mahogany sideboards and steel engravings of the royal family were typical Victorian furnishings. Porchester Terrace is a street of large houses in West London, running down to Bayswater Road and Kensington Gardens.
4. *Rugby*: boys' private school in the Midlands, famous for its cult of fair play and its preparation of the students for public office, either at home (like Ernest Thorburn) or in the colonies.
5. *golden-wedding party*: to celebrate fifty years of marriage.
6. *pinchbeck*: alloy of copper and zinc that resembles gold.
7. *South Kensington . . . tube station*: the Thorburns are hard up and live in a shabby-genteel area, south of the fashionable West End. The tube is the underground.
8. *Cromwell Road . . . the Natural History Museum*: Cromwell Road is a wide street in South Kensington on the corner of which stands the Natural History Museum, built in the 1870s. The Central Hall used to contain many stuffed animals in glass cases.